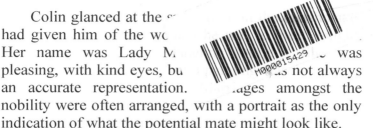

Colin glanced at the ⌐
had given him of the wc
Her name was Lady M.   .⌐ was
pleasing, with kind eyes, bu   ..⌐ not always
an accurate representation.   ..ages amongst the
nobility were often arranged, with a portrait as the only
indication of what the potential mate might look like.

Still, as he searched the room, he believed he saw
someone who looked like the person in the portrait he
held. She stood talking to an older woman who sat on
an unusual-looking chair on wheels. He suspected they
might be related, as both had the same way of smiling.
Their smiles were open and honest, no pretense.

The older woman was frail, her shoulders thin and
rounded. Every few moments she would cough, and
when she did, Lady Madeline's eyes would widen
slightly, but then she would mask her concern with a
smile as she straightened the older woman's long skirts
or brought her tea.

The party was well under way. People gathered in
clusters around the tree, or in groups around the room,
yet Lady Madeline stayed close beside the older
woman.

Colin held the portrait higher, rubbing his thumb
over the woman's lips. The painting of the Lady
Madeline did not do her justice. She was the most
beautiful woman he had ever seen. But he was not here
to fall in love. He did not believe in such fantasies of
the heart. He was here to find a woman who could
break Merlin's Curse.

Praise for Pam Binder

"Pam Binder gracefully weaves elements of humor, magic and romantic tension."

~Publishers Weekly

~*~

Awards
2018 Romantic Times Pioneers of Romance Fiction Award
for helping forge the way for the many subgenres in romance

~

FALLING IN LOVE WITH EMMA was a 2018 finalist in the Desert Rose RWA, Golden Quill Contest

~*~

Books in the Matchmaker Café Series
MATCH MADE IN THE HIGHLANDS
A BRIDE FOR A DAY
FALLING IN LOVE WITH EMMA
THIEF OF HEARTS
CHRISTMAS KNIGHT
IRISH LOVE SONG

Christmas Knight

by

Pam Binder

Matchmaker Café Series
Book Five

This is a work of fiction. Names, characters, places, and incidents are either the product of the author's imagination or are used fictitiously, and any resemblance to actual persons living or dead, business establishments, events, or locales, is entirely coincidental.

Christmas Knight

COPYRIGHT © 2019 by Pam Binder

All rights reserved. No part of this book may be used or reproduced in any manner whatsoever without written permission of the author or The Wild Rose Press, Inc. except in the case of brief quotations embodied in critical articles or reviews.
Contact Information: info@thewildrosepress.com

Cover Art by *Kristian Norris*

The Wild Rose Press, Inc.
PO Box 708
Adams Basin, NY 14410-0708
Visit us at www.thewildrosepress.com

Publishing History
First Fantasy Rose Edition, 2019
Print ISBN 978-1-5092-2798-3
Digital ISBN 978-1-5092-2799-0

Matchmaker Café Series, Book Five
Published in the United States of America

Dedication

To my son, Brock,
who is kind, courageous, and a man of honor

Prologue

Tintagel Castle, England, 1485

Colin Edward Penrose bounded down the stairs two at a time. He had left his father's chamber in the same way he entered: at a dead run. He needed air.

At the bottom of the stairs, the hum of voices rose to greet him. His father had invited over half of Glastonbury, members of the clergy, and the surrounding villages to participate in the Twelfth Night Christmas celebrations. The Great Hall overflowed with guests eating his father's food and drinking his wine.

Colin was not in a festive mood.

His father had given him ultimatums before, and he had learned the hard way they were not hollow threats.

Colin reached the double doors that led outside, but Douglas Channing blocked his path. Sturdy and a head shorter than Colin, Douglas was fair where Colin was dark. They were the same age and had been best friends since the day Douglas had been fostered to Lord Penrose.

"What did your father say?" Douglas said.

"My father demands I wed, or he will declare Henry his heir."

Douglas sucked in his breath. "Your father sounds serious this time."

Colin nodded. "He is not the man he once was. He

has lost the spark in his eyes, as though he is letting go of this world and longs for the next one—the world where he will see my mother again."

Douglas put his hand on Colin's shoulder. "Then you must give him a reason to live. The most important thing to your father is his family. Marry and give him a grandchild."

"You know that is not possible. No woman will marry a Penrose heir." Colin rolled his shoulders and glanced toward the Great Hall. "He said there was a visiting matchmaker attending the celebrations."

Douglas nodded. "That would be Nessa, from the Romani camp. I heard she is the same person who found a match for your father. A matchmaker will make you believe in love."

"I would settle for a wife."

Chapter One

Present day, Seattle, Washington

Colin ducked under a doorway as he followed the Romani matchmaker Nessa into a manor house she said was in Glastonbury, England, but he did not recognize the place, and he had grown up in the area. Her loose-fitting, meadow-green gown, short blonde hair, and heart-shaped face made her look like barely seventeen or eighteen years old, too young for the woman she claimed to be. She'd told him that she had matched his parents almost thirty years ago.

Perhaps he had misunderstood. He had a lot on his mind.

And he had learned long ago that when it came to the Romani and anyone connected with them, it was better not to ask too many questions. They believed in magic and things that could not be explained.

She motioned for him to follow her to a shadowed section of the ballroom. Guests arrived in pairs or groups from an entrance on the far side of the ballroom. Their garments appeared to be in the style of King Arthur, and Nessa had insisted he wear the same style. Sir Thomas Malory had published his book *The Death of Arthur* a few months ago, and it seemed the whole of England had gone mad with trying to recreate Camelot.

The ballroom was half the size of the one at

Tintagel Castle, and although outside the bank of windows the night was as dark as a hangman's heart, inside it looked as though it were lit by a thousand torches. The only visible source of light came from candles that covered a fourteen-foot fir tree positioned in the center of the room and decorated with painted balls of glass. Nessa had said that the people, their clothes, and even the furnishings would seem strange to him. That was an understatement. Where was he?

She also had made him bathe and shave off his beard. An odd request. His father's physician cautioned that frequent baths led to fevers of the lungs. But since he was to meet a potential bride, he did as Nessa had requested. He had refused, however, to give up his sword.

Matchmaker Nessa handed him a palm-sized painted portrait of a woman. "The lady you are to meet has arrived and is standing near the dessert table with her grandmother. Please remember our conversation. Tonight is merely a first meeting to determine if there is an attraction."

Colin interrupted, "I told you that I am not interested in a love match."

Nessa scrunched up her nose. "Yes, you were very clear on that point. As I was saying, you may not care about such things as love, but this woman will. You told me you wanted a wife. This is the first step."

Music blared, and the notes of stringed instruments were so loud that people grumbled and covered their ears. A few feet away, a man dressed in a long tunic waved his hand at the crowd. "Sorry. I'll turn it down."

Within a matter of seconds, the music faded into the background.

Colin rubbed the back of his neck. "Where are the musicians?"

Nessa's expression looked pinched. "Hidden. We hide them here. That's not your worry. Your task is to meet a potential bride. Do not try to be anyone other than yourself, and you'll do fine." She glanced into the crowd. "Remember to smile. One of my sisters is looking for me. I'll check on your progress in a short while."

Colin watched her disappear into the crowded party. She had told him to be himself. He did not understand her statement. Who else would he be? Then she had told him to smile. He smiled. Not often, but he smiled.

Colin glanced at the small portrait the matchmaker had given him of the woman he was to meet tonight. Her name was Lady Madeline Murphy. She was pleasing, with kind eyes, but a painting was not always an accurate representation. Marriages amongst the nobility were often arranged, with a portrait as the only indication of what the potential mate might look like. He had heard that one of the monarchs in Europe had been so enraged when he met his bride for the first time, and realized she looked nothing like the gorgeous woman in the portrait he had been given, that he had ordered the painter imprisoned.

Still, as he searched the room, he believed he saw someone who looked like the person in the portrait he held. She stood talking to an older woman who sat on an unusual-looking chair on wheels. He suspected they might be related, as both had the same way of smiling. Their smiles were open and honest, no pretense.

The older woman was frail, her shoulders thin and

rounded. Every few moments she would cough, and when she did, Lady Madeline's eyes would widen slightly, but then she would mask her concern with a smile as she straightened the older woman's long skirts or brought her tea.

The party was well under way. People gathered in clusters around the tree, or in groups around the room, yet Lady Madeline stayed close beside the older woman.

Colin held the portrait higher, rubbing his thumb over the woman's lips. The painting of the Lady Madeline did not do her justice. She was the most beautiful woman he had ever seen. But he was not here to fall in love. He did not believe in such fantasies of the heart. He was here to find a woman who could break Merlin's Curse.

Chapter Two

Across the room, Madeline's grandmother had fallen asleep in her wheelchair. Madeline lifted a blanket over Gran's lap and pulled up a chair to sit beside her. Madeline brushed lint from her red velvet, low-cut rented gown. She'd chosen a more conservative dress from a catalogue for tonight, but for some reason a mistake had occurred, and this one had appeared in its place, too late to order another.

The mix-up with her dress only proved her belief that tonight would be a total disaster. How could it not? A few weeks ago, this whole fiasco had started when she'd lied to her grandmother. Gran asked if she had a date, and Madeline had said that he was too busy. Of course, there was no boyfriend. Gran had looked sad and disappointed, and Madeline had made it worse by promising to bring her imaginary boyfriend to the party. In full-on panic mode, Madeline had turned to the matchmaker sisters in the Village for help, and tonight she would meet her mystery man for the first time.

She'd given matchmaker Nessa a detailed description of her ideal man, his interests and education level. She wanted the man to be well mannered and athletic as well as tall, dark, and handsome. In other words, she wanted the fantasy.

What had she been thinking? Madeline should be satisfied with her life. She didn't need a man. She was a successful lawyer, with an apartment overlooking Seattle's Puget Sound. That the men she dated didn't stick around for long or believe in monogamy was a different topic. Then there was the added bonus that when she invited someone she was dating to meet her family, they never approved of him. If this matchmaker escort arrangement worked out, however, she wouldn't have to produce a date again until the next holiday season rolled around.

She wanted to believe that she hadn't given up on love, but it was becoming harder and harder to reconcile her experience with any confidence in the emotion. Love seemed to run faster from her than her father's clients ran from the truth.

Madeline straightened and took a deep breath, scanning the crowd for a man who looked out of place. How else could she describe someone who needed a date on Christmas Eve?

Madeline's mother had outdone herself this year. She'd chosen the perfect venue for the Christmas party, and the medieval-themed event had pleased Gran, which made it even better. The matchmaker sisters had transformed their café. A Christmas tree stood in the center of the room. Its branches were covered with electric lights shaped like candles, crystal icicles, and ornaments that were hand-painted with scenes of snow-covered horses with carriages, forest creatures, and English cottages.

Her mother was a wedding and party planner and had requested in the invitations that people wear fourteenth- or fifteenth-century costumes or those reminiscent of King Arthur's Camelot. Gran loved anything in the medieval and Renaissance time periods and had taken first her daughter and then her granddaughter to the annual fairs in Ashland, Oregon.

The venue had also been her mother's idea. The Matchmaker Café was one of the shops located in a quiet little village east of Seattle and close to where her mother worked. The shops were connected by meandering brick paths lined with flowerpots and with trees with twinkling white lights. Tonight, the café's tables and chairs had been replaced with groupings of overstuffed wingback chairs and upholstered loveseats, more befitting to the style of the fifteenth century.

Gran yawned, covering her mouth with her hand. "I must have dozed off. What did I miss?"

Madeline bent down and adjusted a long strand of pearls around her grandmother's neck from where it had hooked over a gold brooch. "Not a thing. Guests are still arriving."

Gran looked better than she had in months. There was more color in her skin, and she walked as though she wasn't in as much pain. She'd had hip surgery a month ago and it had been a success, although the doctor wanted her to be in a wheelchair tonight as a precaution. He didn't want her to fall, as it might cause further damage to the hip before it had a chance to heal properly.

Gran patted Madeline on the sleeve. "Can you see your fella, dear?"

"Not yet." She glanced toward the crowd. From the number of guests so far, it looked like almost everyone on the list had arrived. All she knew about Colin Edward Penrose the Sixth was that he was English and would be wearing a Scottish Thistle pin on his King Arthur-style costume. Since the majority of the men were dressed like King Arthur or his Knights of the Round Table, the matchmaker's description wasn't that helpful.

"I don't think he's arrived yet. He's a visiting teacher from Oxford," Madeline said, repeating the lie she'd rehearsed in her head. "Gran you look amazing," she said in a rush, hoping to change the subject. She hated lying to her grandmother.

Her grandmother beamed, reaching over to squeeze her hand. "As do you. Your dress looks like it was made for you. I remember when you were little you loved pretending you lived in the Renaissance and wanted to be the Queen of England. I was surprised when you became an attorney."

"I love helping people who can't afford a lawyer."

Gran leaned back in her wheelchair and folded her hands neatly in her lap. "You work for that father of yours, and the only clients he has are ones who are richer than Midas."

"I also volunteer for an organization in Seattle that helps those who can't afford an attorney."

Gran harrumphed. "How often do you get to do that? Once or twice every few months? I know your father. He keeps you so busy with his rich clients that you have little time even for yourself. You need to start your own firm." She scooted to the edge of the wheelchair. "Your mother opened a nice little office in this village. If you opened your own law office, you'd be closer to your mother and me. Your room is exactly as you left it."

Madeline helped Gran sit farther back in the chair. "I'm not moving home. I like Seattle, and I have a great apartment."

"If by great you mean cold, dark, and lonely, then I agree."

She loved Gran, but she and her mother were broken records when it came to this subject. Gran had never liked Madeline's father, and that was way before he'd cheated on her mother. He was in the crowd somewhere with his third wife.

Her mother strolled over, looking happier than Madeline had seen her in months. She wore a green velvet gown the same shade as her eyes. She'd been worried about Gran leading up to the hip surgery and had insisted that she move in with her. The women in her family turned worrying into an art form. But in this case, Madeline agreed wholeheartedly. Her mother seemed happier with Gran around and had started dating again.

Her mother squeezed Madeline's hand in much the same way Gran had. They were a family of huggers, Gran liked to say.

"Thank you for looking after Gran. I'll take her over to have a talk with her friends while you see if you can find that man of yours. Gran and I are anxious to meet him."

"He's probably not coming," Madeline said, more disappointed than she cared to admit. It probably had something to do with the ridiculous list she'd given Nessa. Men like Madeline had described didn't exist, or if they did, they certainly didn't need a blind date for Christmas Eve.

"Nonsense," Gran said. "My two girls will find love. All it takes is a leap of faith."

"Gran, you sound like a fortune cookie," Madeline said.

"Darn right," Gran said with a nod. "There are some mighty wise words in those fortune cookies." She smiled at her daughter. "Elizabeth, you should follow your own advice. You asked Madeline to introduce her fella to us, while I've yet to meet yours."

Elizabeth shot Madeline a sly smile and a wink. "Mom, you haven't approved of the last few men I've dated. I'm a little afraid to introduce you to this one."

Gran rolled her eyes. "I don't want you to make the same mistake again is all. I'm a good judge of character. I knew the moment I laid eyes on your father that he was a good man, and he'd tell you the same thing if he were still with us."

"Yes, he would," Elizabeth said as she gave her mother a gentle hug around the shoulders. "How about this idea? I'll leave you with your friends at the dessert table and bring Finnigan over to meet you. He is helping with the music's sound system." With Gran's nod of approval, Elizabeth turned Gran in the direction of the table piled high with pastries and cookies decorated with images of knights, ladies of the court, and the wizard, Merlin.

"Finnigan? What kind of name is Finnigan? Is he Irish?"

Madeline didn't hear her mother's response and lost the rest of the conversation as her mother wheeled Gran toward the dessert table a short distance away.

Behind her, a man cleared his throat. "Begging your pardon, milady. I am Colin Edward Penrose the Sixth. Are you the Lady Madeline?"

Startled, she froze as a thrill of anticipation chased over her arms. The voice was deep and rich, with a thick English accent. She turned slowly, as though in a dream, and had to tilt her head to meet his gaze. His brown eyes hinted of amber and promises that would melt a woman's heart. He looked like he had stepped out of her fantasy vision of how a knight should look. She had to hand it to the matchmaker. She knew what she was doing.

He had broad shoulders and wore a white tunic with gold trim over close-fitting leggings. A leather belt, complete with a sword, rode his hips. The only thing that kept her from swooning was that she didn't want to embarrass herself.

She held out her hand. "Yes, I'm Madeline." Okay, not bad. Her voice was stable and her hand wasn't shaking. So far so good. "It's nice to meet you, Colin."

He inclined his head, then bent to take her hand and kiss it. "Lady Madeline."

"Oh." His breath was warm against her skin, and having her hand kissed the way she'd seen it done in movies sent her thoughts spiraling in a hundred different directions at the same time. He played the role of a chivalrous knight to perfection. If she swooned, would he catch her? *Stop it. You're a high-powered attorney, not a foolish schoolgirl. Besides, this guy is your escort for the evening. He's not real.*

"Would you mind if we bypassed the titles? You can call me Madeline, and may I call you Colin?"

He seemed to ponder her remark and bowed again. "As you wish."

Good grief, now he was quoting lines from the movie *The Princess Bride*. She sort of liked it, but her parents, especially her father, might find it over the top and start asking too many questions. How did you tell a guy to ease off on the good manners without sounding rude?

"Where in England are you from?"

"Cornwall. I live at our ancestral home at Tintagel Castle."

This guy kept getting better and better. She was mesmerized by his deep voice and English accent, and he had done his research. Tintagel Castle was believed to be the birthplace of King Arthur.

Madeline winked conspiratorially as she said, "Tintagel Castle. Good one. Too bad in real life it's a ruin."

His eyebrows knitted together. "It is true that battles have left their mark, but it is hardly a ruin."

The dessert table buckled. Plates crashed to the ground, and cream-filled cookies, slices of chocolate cake, and frosted donuts splattered to the ground.

Startled guests screamed and scattered to get out of the way or jumped over the fallen desserts. Gran stood quickly, and her wheelchair rolled out of her reach. She extended her arms for balance and windmilled the air. She looked like a deer caught in a car's headlights, not knowing what to do next.

Colin and Madeline raced toward Gran.

Colin reached Gran first and caught her in his arms just as she started to fall. The table collapsed completely, and Colin shielded Gran with his body from the falling debris, then carried her to the nearest sofa. He removed his tunic and used it as a pillow as he placed it under Gran's head.

Out of breath, Madeline's mother knelt down next to Colin. She cradled her mother's hands in hers. "Are you all right?"

"Right as rain," Gran said, beaming at Colin.

"Thanks to this nice young man. He swooped in like a knight in shining armor. Thank you."

"You are most welcome," Colin said, with a slight bow.

Madeline's hand shook as she stroked her Gran's snow-white hair off her forehead, grateful Colin had made it in time to catch her grandmother before she fell. "Yes, thank you, Colin. Gran, we should take you to the hospital, just to make sure you're okay."

Nessa, her face pinched with worry, shouldered her way through the crowd gathered around Gran. "This is terrible. Are you all right?"

Gran frowned. "Oh, for heaven's sake. I didn't fall. Why is everyone making such a fuss?"

"It's true that you didn't fall, Mom," Elizabeth said, "but you could have. It was very scary, and it's because we love you that we want to make sure you're okay. It's just a precaution."

"Do you have a carriage?" Colin said, looking toward Madeline. "Or a horse I could borrow? I will bring a physician to your grandmother."

She and her mother were grateful Colin had prevented Gran from falling, but he was taking his role as a knight too far. No doubt Colin was an actor hired by Nessa. So much for meeting her soulmate. For a few minutes, she'd almost believed her fantasy man had come true.

"We don't have a horse. We have a car," Madeline said with a bite to her tone.

Gran reached up and patted Colin on the cheek. "I like this one, Madeline. You should keep him."

Chapter Three

One year later

A plastic Christmas wreath with a tired-looking red bow hung from the judge's bench in the courtroom where Madeline waited for the ruling on her client's prenuptial case. Her client wanted upheld the prenuptial he'd signed with his soon-to-be ex-wife.

Madeline, lead counsel for her father's family law practice, held her breath, grateful no one had put up a Christmas tree. Christmas trees reminded her of last year's party and the man who did what most men did when they met her—they ran from her when they learned how successful she was at her job, or as in the case of her ex-boyfriend, they cheated.

Gran had called Colin a knight in shining armor. Some knight. He'd disappeared with Nessa right as Madeline and her mother were leaving for the hospital with Gran. She'd met him only that one time. Why couldn't she get him out of her mind?

The bailiff announced that the judge was about to make his ruling. She buried thoughts of Colin and leaned forward as the judge took his place in the courtroom. The judge looked haggard; his gaze focused on his folder. Litigating to uphold prenuptials or to dissolve a marriage during the holiday season was rough on everyone. This was the time of miracles and happily-ever-afters, not the time when lives were torn apart.

The wreath on the judge's desk quivered as he settled behind his bench and flipped open his file, bringing down his gavel. "The prenuptial stands."

He went on, explaining more of the details, but his words were drowned out by the congratulations from her client's side of the court. She'd won. Moans of disbelief broke out on the plaintiff's side and cast a shadow over the room.

Madeline let out her breath. The verdict was in, and Madeline had won.

So why did she feel as though she had lost?

She collected her papers while her father congratulated their client. Madeline felt mentally and physically exhausted. The eighty-hour work week for trial attorneys was a myth. It was closer to one hundred. She stretched her lips into a smile because her father would notice otherwise, and reached for her pens, wondering why she didn't share her father's enthusiasm.

Each case was harder than the last, which was strange, as they all seemed to have a similar basis, which should have made it easier, not the opposite. During the initial interviews, the client told his or her history, and some brought wedding and holiday pictures. In the beginning, there were always wedding, honeymoon, and vacation smiles, with couples sitting close to each other. As years passed, smiles faded, couples sat farther and farther apart, or were absent from the photos altogether. With each picture, the chasm grew, and the longer they allowed it to grow unchecked, the more bitter and expensive the divorce.

When there were children, it could get worse.

By the time the couples reached the Murphy law firm, the damage was irreconcilable. Each case Madeline tried and won confirmed her position that she was glad to be single.

She kept her head down and concentrated on shuffling folders into her briefcase. Her part was over and with it the adrenaline rush. She mentally reviewed the stack of cases on her desk at the office. It would be another all-nighter, with deli takeout, a glass of wine, and an old movie as a reward.

Her father beamed, congratulating the client and pumping the man's hand. He often told his clients that he and his daughter were the perfect combination. His daughter loved going in for the kill, and he loved reaping the spoils of war. She hated the picture he painted of her. She wasn't heartless. She was doing her job.

She told her friends and family that she took these cases in stride, like battles to be won or lost. But in war there were always casualties, and that was taking its toll. Being good at what you did was sometimes a curse.

Madeline prided herself on the ability to distance herself emotionally from her cases. At least that's what she told her colleagues. The truth wasn't as clear cut. So why had this case hit her so hard? Why had she secretly hoped she'd lose? Why had she written another letter of resignation to her father?

She shoved the last folder into her briefcase, but it wouldn't slide into place. She reached inside to adjust the papers and discovered the cause. Wedged in at the bottom was the invitation to her mother's wedding in

England on Christmas Eve, a week from today. In flowing cursive, Gran had handwritten an unusual request across the invitation.

Against all the rules she herself had put into place when she first accepted her father's offer to join his law firm, she glanced toward the plaintiff's side of the court. The woman, her arm around her young daughter, stared straight ahead, while the attorney explained what would happen next.

Madeline had noticed from the beginning how much the woman looked like her mother, with her oval-shaped face and straight auburn hair. Madeline knew the woman's attorney had insisted she wear a conservative gray suit for the proceedings; however, the woman's individuality shone through. Tucked under the sleeves of her jacket were stacks of multi-colored stone bracelets. Her daughter was about the same age Madeline had been when her parents divorced.

Madeline's legs buckled. Shaking, she sank down in her chair to catch her breath.

A woman wearing a dark navy suit and hair pulled up in a bun appeared at her side. "Are you all right? You look pale. The proceedings were over, and a nice man let me into the courtroom. You are so busy, and I know time is of the essence."

"Ah, Lady Roselyn from the Matchmaker Café," Madeline said, taking a deep breath. "I'm fine. I haven't eaten is all." Her fingers fumbled to close her briefcase. "You got my message?"

Lady Roselyn nodded and sat in the vacant chair next to Madeline. "Your mother is marrying on Christmas Eve, and your grandmother insists that you invite the gentleman you brought to last year's party.

I'm assuming they didn't know my sister, Nessa, arranged the match?"

"That is correct," Madeline said. "I kept meaning to tell them that I'd broken up with my fictitious boyfriend, but for some reason I never got around to it."

"And now it is too late and they want you to bring him to your mother's wedding," Lady Roselyn said.

Madeline propped her elbow on the table and leaned her head on her hand. "I've dug myself into a hole, haven't I? I should tell them we broke up."

"Except you told me you've already agreed you'd bring him."

Madeline leaned back in her chair. "I'm a people pleaser. What can I say? Can you just hire the guy again? Gran insists I invite Colin."

Lady Roselyn's lips drew together in a straight line. "You have the wrong impression of what we do. We're not an escort service. We find a person's soulmate."

"Nessa said the same thing. Colin seemed so perfect, as though Nessa conjured him for me out of thin air."

Lady Roselyn raised an eyebrow. "Indeed. In any event, I'm having difficulty locating him. That's why I'm here. I need to ask you a few more questions, if I may."

The people had cleared the courtroom, some to celebrate and others to pick up the pieces. Her destination was her office and her takeout. "I have time," she said to Lady Roselyn. "Ask your questions."

Lady Roselyn pulled out a notepad and reviewed her notes. "Other than his name, what else do you know about Colin?"

Madeline secured the latch on her briefcase. She'd gone over the conversation she'd had with Colin hundreds of times. She'd thought he was just a stiff Englishman, playing a part as her boyfriend. But something didn't ring true.

"The person Nessa arranged to act as my boyfriend introduced himself as Colin Edward Penrose the Sixth, which I thought was a good touch, and he remained in the character of a knight the whole time. He even told me that he actually lived at Tintagel Castle. I remembered the name, as I'm a Camelot geek, and legend claims Tintagel was the birthplace of King Arthur. I'd seen photos of the castle ruins and hadn't remembered reading that it had been restored. I planned to ask him more about it, but that was when Gran almost fell. Afterward he and Nessa disappeared, and I didn't see him again."

Lady Roselyn chewed on the side of her pen. "Are you sure he said he *lived* at that castle? Maybe he meant the surrounding area."

Madeline pushed her chair back from the table. "It's possible. I only talked to him for a short time, and then Gran's near fall happened. We took her to be checked over, while he went off with Nessa. I should get back to work. I have a long night ahead of me. If you can't find Colin, I can figure something out to tell my grandmother."

Lady Roselyn glanced over her notes. "I want to help you if I can. Colin certainly made quite an impression on your grandmother." She paused. "What about you? Would you like to see him again?"

Madeline pulled her briefcase onto her lap. "The truth is that I can't seem to get him out of my mind. Is that good or bad?"

Lady Roselyn reached over to pat Madeline's hand. "That is very good. I will do my best. Now, is there anything else you remember? The smallest detail could help."

Madeline stood and slung her messenger-style briefcase over her shoulder. "There was one odd remark he made. He wanted to know if we had a carriage, or a horse he could borrow so he could find a physician for Gran. Gran got a big kick out of it. My mother and I thought he'd carried his role as a knight to the extreme. Looking back, he seemed out of place, somehow. Or I could have imagined that he felt uncomfortable."

Lady Roselyn turned pale as she stood and leaned on the chair. She glanced over her shoulder and lowered her voice. "Do you know the type of man you asked Nessa to find for you?"

"Let me think. That was over a year ago, but I remember I told her how much I liked all the stories about King Arthur, and that it would be great if she could find someone for me who shared those interests. I remember we also talked about Merlin and his sword, Excalibur. Does that help?"

Lady Roselyn pushed the chair under the table. It scraped against the floor as she said, "Very helpful."

"Do you think you can find Colin?"

"That's a very good question."

Chapter Four

Glastonbury, England—Fifteenth Century

The winter storm built overhead, bruising the English skies and sending waves against the rock walls. Colin raced his horse, Dragon, along the edge of the cliff toward Tintagel Castle as though chased by the hounds of hell.

The battle he fought for control of Dozmary Pool in Cornwall had already cooled and the mercenaries had fled by the time he received the message that his father had fallen from his horse. Colin put his lieutenant in charge in the event the mercenaries returned. King Arthur's sword, Excalibur, was believed to rest at the bottom of Dozmary Pool, and Colin was not the only one who sought to possess it.

When they secured Dozmary they had searched the shallow pool and found no trace of a sword, only bits of pottery and bones. That meant there was only one other place it could be, and he would need an army to steal it. He did not want the sword for the power it could wield against an enemy; he wanted it to break the curse Merlin had placed on his family.

Even if he did find Excalibur before the deadline on Christmas Eve, there was no guarantee he would find a woman willing to risk marrying into his family.

Last year he had given in to his father's demands

that he elicit the help of the matchmaker Nessa. She claimed she could find a woman who could break Merlin's Curse, the "woman out of time" that Merlin had mentioned. To do so, however, he would have to kidnap her. But when he met Madeline he had backed away. He was not a perfect man, but he would not kidnap a woman, no matter that his inheritance was at stake.

While the Lady Madeline cared for her grandmother, he had sought Nessa and demanded she return him home. In the brief time he had spent with the lady he had felt an attraction, and that scared him worse than a pack of hungry wolves. Marriage to a Penrose could not be about love. It was about duty and sacrifice. He was grateful he would never see her again. Love was not for him, even though he could never stop thinking of her.

Rain released from the sky as shadows deepened.

He leaned over Dragon's neck. "We are almost at Tintagel, old friend," he said over the clap of thunder.

Dragon's hooves kicked up loose turf and pebbles that tumbled over the cliff into the boiling waves as Colin neared the drawbridge. It was down, and the iron gates were pulled skyward like the gaping jaws of a predatory beast.

Colin drew back in concern at the open gates and lack of caution. Attacks were common. It was not like his father to drop his guard. Colin left the dirt path to enter the castle. His horse's hooves thundered over the wooden drawbridge, then clattered when they struck the cobblestone tunnel leading to the castle's entrance.

Once inside, decorations honoring the twelve nights leading to Christmas transformed the stone walls.

Boughs of holly and ivy decorated either side of the gate, and the sound of music rose above the moans of the wind and crashing waves. This year, as a precaution, his father had forbidden the use of mistletoe. They were already under the scrutiny of the church in Glastonbury because of Merlin's Curse. Mistletoe was connected to the old religions and pagan fertility festivals and thus forbidden by the church. Colin thought it superstitious nonsense, but he knew that the older his father grew, the more he seemed to fear Judgment Day.

Colin slowed Dragon's pace to a walk. Two guards snapped to attention on his approach, hiding their tankards of ale behind their backs. It was the week leading to Christmas Eve, a time of celebration and good will toward men. His father allowed all those within the castle walls to join in the festival atmosphere, believing that the world also adhered to the tradition of peace during this sacred time.

Colin dismounted, concerned by the disregard for more security along the wall and the raised gate. If an enemy attacked, those within the castle would be at their mercy. He had argued this point with his father before and gained nothing for his effort. His father lived in the past, a time when the rules of chivalry reigned. The battle Colin had fought a few days prior proved those days were long gone, if they ever existed in the first place.

"Yer lordship," the taller of the two guards said with a bow of respect and a slur of his words.

"My father…is he…?"

The tall man motioned over his shoulder. "The lord is as well as can be expected. He is in his chambers."

Colin let out a breath of relief, yet caught the glance the guards exchanged. His father might be alive, but not for long, their expressions seemed to say. He tossed his horse's reins to the man and raced up the outer stairs.

"Did ye win the battle, Sire?" the shorter man shouted.

"A battle is never won," Colin said, pausing only briefly, "as long as hate remains in men's hearts."

****

Once inside, Colin took the stairs to his father's chamber two at a time. He swore under his breath. His father had been injured in a hunting accident, and yet Twelfth Night celebrations raged in the Great Hall.

The only detail the messenger knew was that his father had been thrown off his horse and was in serious condition. Why his father had felt compelled to hunt in the dead of winter, let alone ride a spirited animal at his age, was beyond him. But telling his father, Lord Penrose, with lands in Scotland, Wales, and Ireland, that he should no longer ride, would not end well, even if the person who told him was his only child.

Colin pushed open the double doors to his father's chamber and was hit with a blast of warm air despite the winter storm that raged outside the castle walls. Windows were shrouded with thick embroidered curtains, the fireplace gave off waves of heat, and candles were crammed on every available space like a church on feast day.

His father was propped on feather pillows against the headboard of a four-poster bed, with two serving women in attendance. He looked in a dark mood. "Is that you, son?" His voice was threadbare as he peered around the women.

"Yes, I am here, Father. Save your strength." Had his father grown thinner since Colin had been away? His voice less steady?

His father waved the women out of the room, with instructions for them to send for the matchmaker Nessa's sister, Fiona. He then motioned for his son to join him. The women avoided Colin's gaze, keeping their distance as they rushed past him into the hallway. He had that effect on women. These were superstitious times, and as the Penrose heir, he was living proof that dark magic existed. He prayed finding Excalibur would change his fate.

Colin waited until the women had left the chamber and shut the door behind them before approaching his father's bedside. Colin kept his hands locked behind his back. His father disapproved of shows of emotion, believing them a sign of weakness. "What did the physicians say?"

His father took a shallow breath of air and groaned as though gripped in a wave of pain. "Broken bones. Ribs. The physicians are fools and near bled me dry with their bloodsucking leeches." The attempt to sit up straighter ended with another moan and a whispered, "Blasted horse."

Colin reached out toward his father to make him more comfortable by fluffing the pillows and pulling the blanket over his chest. His father surprised him with a pat on his hand.

When Colin hesitated at the sudden show of affection, his father cleared his throat and snapped, "Where's my wine?"

Colin tamped down the conflict of emotions racing

through him and reached for a pewter goblet on a table by the bedside. His father's unexpected show of affection, so desired when Colin was a young lad, troubled him now. They said a man changed when he feared death.

He ignored the shiver of dread. He believed his father was invincible, a force as strong and formidable as the walls of Tintagel Castle. Then his father's favorite quotation repeated in his thoughts like a Gregorian chant. *Even the most fortified castles crumble and turn to dust.*

Colin placed one hand on his father's shoulder and lifted the wine to his mouth to help him drink. His father took a generous gulp. Red wine spilled out the corners of his mouth like rivulets of blood. Taking the goblet, Colin wiped his father's chin and eased him back down against the pillows.

"The physicians want me to order my horse, Magic, killed," his father said. "I'm considering it."

Colin's dread increased, and his blood ran as cold as the storm outside at the unusual request. His horse, Dragon, had sired Magic. It was true that from the moment of Magic's birth the animal had tried to escape. It had a temper and a mind of its own that refused to be tamed. But Colin and his father loved the beast. To consider ending its life was unlike his father. He worried something else troubled his father, to take such a dramatic turn. "You will feel differently once you are healed. There is no horse that loves the hunt as much as Magic."

"And yet, according to the doctor, it tried to murder its lord."

"Father…" The word burst from Colin as a chill

chased up his spine. How bad were his father's injuries? His eyes looked sunken, his skin pale and drawn. When had he grown old and tired? Colin shook away the image and cleared his throat. "The physician is mistaken. You have survived worse injuries on the field of battle."

"Perhaps." His father turned to lock his gaze on Colin. "This accident has forced me to face my mortality. Not a pleasant task, might I add. Life is fragile and death all too final. If I die, you alone stand against those who would steal our lands. You are reckless with your life. You place yourself on the frontline of battle when you could direct the strategies of war from a secure location miles away."

Colin's hands clenched at the familiar criticism. "My men deserve a leader who fights at their side."

His father pounded his fist on the bedside table, toppling over the wine. The pewter goblet crashed to the wooden floor, staining the rushes blood-red. "Enough. If you die without an heir, your cousin, Henry Blackstone, will inherit our lands. You must wed on your thirtieth birthday, this Christmas Eve, and produce an heir within the year. If you fail, I must declare someone else heir, or risk Henry challenging you in the courts."

Colin balled his fists as his temper rose. "I carry this weight on my shoulders as well, Father. Henry is a drunkard and gambles as though money were as plentiful as leaves on trees. But no woman will agree to marry me, knowing the consequences. You saw the reactions of your servant women, and they have known me all my life. And even if we found a woman foolish enough, I would turn her away."

The tone of his father's voice was a match to his son's. "You are not unlike that miserable horse who tossed me to the frozen ground. Stubborn and unreasonable."

"I will not force a woman against her will. A woman who marries a Penrose dies in childbirth. How many will be sacrificed to Merlin's Curse so that we can retain our lands?"

Silence draped like a cloak over the chamber. Some believed that to speak of the curse aloud was to invoke its wrath tenfold. But once said, the damage had been done. Colin picked up the fallen goblet, refilled it with wine, and set it back in place on the table.

"If Excalibur existed…" His father swallowed and settled back against the pillows, sinking into them until he looked small and frail. "I wish… You think me a monster for insisting you wed," his father continued. "Worse, you blame me for your mother's death. I loved her. I believed I had solved the first part of the curse's riddle that instructed a Penrose man to marry a woman out of time. Our ancestors believed the riddle meant that a prospective Penrose bride must be almost past the age of childbearing. The matchmaker Nessa disagreed and convinced me that there was another interpretation."

The phrase had been burned into Colin's memory, and generations of Penrose men had puzzled over its meaning, never solving the riddle. Colin had never known his mother, yet he mourned the loss and wondered how his life, and the choices he made, would have been different if shaped by a mother's touch. Would he be more willing to love? The image of Madeline as she cared for her grandmother appeared.

As quickly as they rose in his thoughts, he ordered them down. He could never see her again, no matter how he wished things were different.

Colin's jaw tightened. "A woman out of time is only part of the equation, Father," Colin said, his tone hard as stone. "One of our ancestors stole Excalibur, and we are tasked with returning it to the Lady of the Lake or we shall watch more of our women die."

His father threw his wine decanter in Colin's direction. Again wine splattered over the floor like blood. "You think I am not aware of Excalibur and the part it plays in our fate? We have spent generations searching for it, and if it ever existed, it is lost to the ages. We cannot continue this fruitless quest. The Penrose line must continue. You must wed."

Colin's voice rang flat. "My mother died hours after I took my first breath in this world. Until I possess Excalibur, I will not take a woman to my bed."

His father's face drained of color. "I see the judgment in your eyes. You think me heartless. I know full well the hour my Catherine died. I did what I did for our family. Get out. I never want to see you again."

Chapter Five

Present Day

Lady Roselyn stormed into the empty Matchmaker Café. Thankfully, she'd had the foresight to ask Bridget to close early today. The last thing she needed were potential clients while they tried to sort out this mess. After talking to Madeline, she suspected Nessa had brought a man from the past to the Christmas Eve party last year. There were so many violations of their matchmaking code she didn't know where to begin.

"Bridget! Where are you? We have to pack. I made reservations on a flight that leaves in the morning."

Bridget walked out of the kitchen, drying her hands. "Where are we going? And why are we taking a plane? We could open a door and reach our destination much faster."

Lady Roselyn tried to unwind the scarf from around her neck and only managed to cinch it tighter. "We are traveling like normal people. The rules around here have been too lax of late. Matchmakers are not allowed to travel for pleasure. We're going to a wedding in Glastonbury because I have to talk with Nessa."

"Let me help you with your scarf," Bridget said, as she worked on the knot around Lady Roselyn's throat. "You're talking about Elizabeth's wedding to Finnegan

O'Doul. How is Nessa involved?"

"You're making the scarf tighter. I can't breathe."

"Then stop fidgeting and hold still. What has Nessa to do with Elizabeth's wedding?"

"It's not about Elizabeth but her daughter, Madeline. Were you aware that Nessa has been freelancing?" Without waiting for Bridget's response, Lady Roselyn grabbed a pair of shears on the table and cut her scarf free of her neck. She rubbed her throat. "It seems our Nessa provided a match for Elizabeth's daughter at last year's Christmas Eve party."

Bridget picked up the ends of the scarf that had floated to the ground. "Why do I have the feeling that was a bad thing?"

"Calling what happened a bad thing is an understatement. I didn't know anything about Nessa's match until Madeline called me last week. She asked me to find the man Nessa had matched for her. When I hit a dead end, I met with Madeline this morning to see if she had any more information about him, other than his name and description."

Bridget looped the ends of the scarf over a chair. "And…"

"And the man's name is Colin Edward Penrose the Sixth. Madeline said he told her that he lives at Tintagel Castle."

"Tintagel is a ruin."

"It's a ruin in the twenty-first century, not the fifteenth."

Bridget stumbled and sat abruptly in the chair. "Oh, no. How did she manage to send Colin forward without our knowledge?"

"That is only one of the problems. Do you

recognize the name?"

"It does sound familiar for some reason," Bridget said.

"That's because there is a big, fat curse attached to it, and I believe Nessa is involved somehow. The real question is how she managed to bring Colin forward without the help of another matchmaker. She would have needed another matchmaker back in Colin's time, to ensure the time-travel door opened properly."

"Isn't Tintagel Castle near Glastonbury?" Bridget said.

"The two places are approximately two hundred miles apart is all," Lady Roselyn said. "Why do you ask?"

"Because our sister Fiona and her new husband, Liam, are honeymooning in that area. It was Nessa's suggestion."

Chapter Six

The chrome-and-glass interior of Madeline's corner office at the Murphy law firm mirrored the view of the Seattle skyline. But that was not her favorite aspect of the scene. Between the buildings, Puget Sound shone like liquid silver in the morning light. A ferryboat left the dock on its journey to one of the San Juan Islands. She wished she had the courage to buy a ticket and not care where the adventure unfolded, only that it would take her far away.

Madeline poised her pen over the signature line of the letter she'd addressed to her father. Her letter of resignation would feel like a betrayal of trust to him. Once she signed the letter, he might not give her a second chance. She sat back in her chair. Amend that last thought. Her father didn't believe in second chances.

When her parents were married, her mother had tricked her father into going to a marriage counselor. He'd thought he was meeting a CEO of a Fortune Five Hundred company. Madeline had never been sure if her father was mad at the deception or that someone else, even a professional therapist, knew that he wasn't perfect. A week later, he had filed for divorce.

Madeline could make the case that she'd done a great job and made a lot of money for his firm and needed a break. She'd attended the University of

Washington's law school with the goal of changing the world. The only worlds she'd changed were the ones she ripped apart in divorce proceedings.

If she took a sabbatical from the practice of law, she might gain perspective and want to return. Her father would counter that she'd received an outrageously high salary, a corner office, and a company car. Any lawyer would jump at the chance to fill her shoes.

A knock on the door had her scrambling to shove the letter into the side drawer of her desk. It floated onto the book her mother had given her last Christmas. A replica of the original *The Death of Arthur*, written in fourteen hundred eighty-five. She'd wanted to display it on her bookshelf but knew her father frowned on personal items in the workplace. She compromised. She locked it where he couldn't find it.

She locked her drawer as her father opened the door—as usual, not waiting for her permission to enter. "We didn't finish our conversation," her father began. "I want you to attend your mother's wedding."

Madeline reached for a folder on a stack of papers. "I have too much work to do, and besides, Mother and Gran wanted me to bring a date." She declined to add that they had someone specific in mind. Madeline had thought that working with her father would bring them closer together. It had only driven them further apart. Her pen ran out of ink, and she reached for another. "Mother will understand if I don't attend the wedding."

"I doubt that."

For once she agreed with her father.

"I applaud your mother for insisting you bring a date. It's time you were married. Marriage suggests stability, and your mother wants grandchildren. The partners keep asking me about your relationship status. I talked with Timothy Cunningham, and he's willing to forget about the past differences you two had and give it another try. He's up for partner," he added, as though that would seal the deal in his favor.

It had the opposite effect.

Madeline gripped the pen in her hand. "Past differences?" she repeated. "Timothy cheated on me…a lot, and I venture to say that he only offered himself up as my date to win points with you and the other partners." Her father hadn't moved or said a word. Unusual for him. He had an opinion on everything. "Dad, what is this really about?"

As though her words had released him, he strode toward her, depositing a plain vanilla folder on her desk. "You have to go to your mother's wedding. It's for the good of the firm. Please read the contract."

Her mother's name was typed on the folder's label. Considering this had something to do with her mother, the folder should have been in a lavender shade, or better yet, splashed with roses or an image of a castle. She remembered when she was in grade school, she'd given her mother a calendar with a different castle for each month. That same year, her mother had given her a similar calendar. Since then it had been their tradition to exchange castle calendars.

The jolt of memory of her mother's hurt expression when a college-bound Madeline had announced that she was too old for castle calendars took Madeline off guard.

Her father was uncharacteristically quiet as Madeline flipped open the folder and skimmed the contract. Several of the pages contained her mother's sprawling signature on a line next to her father's pinched script. Madeline looked up abruptly. "Mother is a shareholder? How did I not know that?"

Her father shrugged. "It was her idea to keep it a secret, and at the time I thought it a sound one. Your mother was a skilled defense attorney and a shrewd businesswoman. She helped me build the firm into the success it is today."

A shadow flickered around her father's expression. He'd given her mother a compliment. A chink in his armor, perhaps?

"Your mother gave that all up to open that little business of hers. I'll never understand why." He moved the folder closer to Madeline.

And the father she knew was back.

Her teeth clenched, Madeline thought about reminding her father that her mother's "little business," as he liked to call it, was the most successful of its kind in the Seattle metropolitan area. She didn't bother. Her father was stuck in his reality. He wouldn't change.

"Your mother is getting married," her father continued, "and the board is nervous. When you attend your mother's wedding, we want you to persuade her to sign these papers, signing her shares over to me."

"What difference does it make after all this time? Obviously, Mother hasn't cared how you have run the firm in the past, so why the urgency now?"

"Your mother is marrying a lawyer. I think they call them solicitors in Europe. How long do you think it will be until her new husband worms his way into our business?"

Madeline glanced at the locked drawer that housed

her letters of resignation. "I will deliver the folder. I will not try to talk my mother into signing. This is between the two of you. If you don't mind, I have a few things I need to do before I leave for the airport. I have a car service to order and a plane to book."

"It's already taken care of. I hear that your mother is doing a themed wedding. She could never get me to dress up in those ridiculous clothes." He looked toward the window that faced the city skyline. "Have you met the man your mother is marrying?"

Her father's voice had softened to a tone she remembered from long ago. It held a touch of regret and something else.

"I met him at last year's Christmas Eve party. He came with us when we took Gran to the hospital after she almost fell." Madeline paused. Her father was stalling. "Would you like me to give Mother a message?"

He straightened. "Just tell her to sign the papers."

Chapter Seven

Tintagel Castle—Fifteenth Century

Inside Tintagel Castle, minstrels played their instruments while a roasted wild boar was presented to the guests, receiving a round of applause. Matchmaker Fiona McBride, standing next to her new husband, Liam, felt her stomach churn. The sight and smell of the boar had turned her stomach. She held her hand to her mouth as her stomach roiled traitorously.

"Are you all right?" Liam asked.

She swallowed and nodded, averting her gaze from the wild boar. "In hindsight, my becoming a vegetarian before we time-traveled to the carnivore-loving fifteenth century was a bad idea. Why did we come here again?"

"King Arthur."

She gave him a weak smile. "King Arthur," she repeated with a nod.

She and Liam were on their honeymoon, traveling throughout the British Isles, and had been invited to the Yule celebrations by a mutual friend. They'd considered declining, until they learned the castle was Tintagel, the birthplace of King Arthur. The opportunity to learn more about the romantic tales of Camelot, the Knights of the Round Table, and the magical Isle of Avalon seemed the perfect ending for their trip through England. She also had wanted to delay her return home and the confrontation with her sisters. They wouldn't understand why she no longer wanted to be a matchmaker. But was that true?

Feeling warm, she wiped moisture from her brow. "I'm not that hungry. Can we go to our room?" With Liam's nod, she put her hand over his arm as he led her from the stench of cooking meat.

"You haven't mentioned a word about the topic that consumes everyone's conversation," Liam said.

"You're talking about Merlin's Curse."

Liam nudged Fiona in the shoulder. "And you can't tell me that you aren't intrigued with the riddle of Merlin's Curse. Colin must marry and have an heir, or lose his inheritance. But that crafty old wizard added a twist. The woman must be out of time or she will die in childbirth. Everyone thought the riddle meant that the lords of Tintagel must marry a woman who was older, and thus running out of time to have a child. Merlin must have known that no one would figure out that he was talking about time travel."

"We can't be certain. Even so, I feel that my sister Nessa is involved somehow and believes the same thing. She pushed hard to make sure we came here. Perhaps she wanted us here to help Colin."

"I know that look, wife. What are you thinking?"

"The young lord has honor. He has refused to marry precisely because his wife would die. That is commendable and tragic. There has to be something we can do."

Liam frowned at his wife. "Matchmaking is not a simple matter. In addition, we match couples. We aren't in the business of arranged marriages."

41

"That's not one hundred percent true. Have you forgotten the match we made in Inverness?"

"I stand corrected. What exactly are you proposing?"

"I intend to find a match for Colin with a woman from the future."

"Is that all, wife? What about world peace?"

"We will tackle that next," Fiona said with a smile.

He heaved a sigh. "Need I remind you that we are on our honeymoon, and you agreed to consider giving up matchmaking?"

She avoided his gaze. She had said she would consider that possibility. When she'd spoken those words, she'd felt overwhelmed with her matchmaking responsibilities and had wanted a break. She had wondered what it would be like to live a normal life and work at a job that started at nine in the morning and ended at five. A job with weekends off, and a set number of vacation days. After months away from matchmaking, she discovered she missed it.

"I know what I said about matchmaking. We could consider this my last hurrah, with a bonus of ending a terrible curse. Win. Win."

Liam eyed Fiona as though considering what she'd said, yet not believing a word. "You have a point. But how would we even contact your sisters to start the process of finding Colin a match? There is the issue of a time-travel door. Nessa told us when we arrived in Glastonbury that the enchanted doors at Tintagel only open in the twenty-first century to the castle ruins. If I want to reach your sisters, I'll have to go to Glastonbury."

Fiona turned her gaze toward her handsome

husband and realized she was smiling at him. She knew him so well. His words to the contrary, the sparkle in his dark eyes, and his questions regarding time-travel doors, told her he was as intrigued with solving the mystery as she was. They were both romantics at heart.

She'd known Liam most of her life. They were both hereditary matchmakers, and their families had betrothed them to each other when they were very young. Their families had been matchmakers for hundreds of years and had developed arranged marriages from the theory that if a couple didn't have to worry about their love life, they could concentrate better on the love lives of others. She had rebelled against her arranged marriage and had delayed the wedding day time after time.

Liam had been patient and had told her that she was worth the wait. She stood on tiptoes to kiss him on the cheek. "Thank you."

He grinned. "For what?"

"For being as big a romantic as I am. You want to help Colin as much as I do."

"What you are proposing has never been done. We are attempting to break a curse devised by the greatest wizard of all time."

"Doing the impossible is what we do."

Liam bent down to brush a kiss against Fiona's neck. "I love you. A kiss before you send me into the cold night?"

"There is time and our room nearby." She leaned into his strong arms, sighing as he wrapped her in an embrace. She touched his lips with the tips of her fingers. "Thank you again."

His eyebrows drew together as he chuckled low.

"I'll gladly take your thanks, my love, but for what do I deserve your praise?"

"For not giving up on us. You were so patient. How did you know that despite my protests I loved you with all my heart?"

He smiled and kissed her. "I'm a matchmaker. We know things."

Her heart warmed in the embrace of the man she loved as she lifted on tiptoes to deepen the kiss. Tonight, she'd planned to tell Liam the news that they were going to have a child. Overhearing the young lord and his father discussing Merlin's Curse changed the timing of her announcement. Once she told Liam about her pregnancy, she would be forbidden to time travel. Time travel was too dangerous for the baby and expectant mother. Liam might also petition that she refrain from matchmaking until after the baby was born.

She drew back and gazed into Liam's eyes, resting her hand on her belly. She didn't want to take any chances either. "I was thinking more of you going alone while I stay behind and suggest to our young lord that there might be other interpretations to the curse. Before you leave, we can go over the qualities we think our young lord looks for in a wife."

"The knight is from the Middle Ages. I doubt he's given it much thought."

"I refuse to believe your assessment. Everyone wants to find their soulmate. Love is timeless."

"Love might be timeless, but what you are proposing is to match a fifteenth-century knight with a twenty-first-century woman. That might work in romance novels. I'm not sure it works in real life."

"I have confidence that you and my sisters will find him a match. This young lord already behaves differently than the other Neanderthals, as you call them. He'd rather give up his inheritance than risk the certain death of the woman he'd marry. Principle over money. That is a very attractive quality."

"Dear wife, you are a hopeless romantic."

Fiona smiled. "Most people would think that is a good quality in a matchmaker."

"Those people would be correct." Liam grew serious. "I don't like leaving you alone. Be careful, especially when it comes to talking about time travel. Someone might think you're a witch, and in this century, they burn or hang witches."

"I must stay and make sure Colin is in Glastonbury when the time comes. I'm not a witch. I'm a matchmaker."

Liam shook his head slowly. "There are people in this century who won't see the distinction."

Chapter Eight

Liam had ridden through the night until he reached Glastonbury, England. Fiona had given him the location of the door he'd need to travel forward to the twenty-first century. While stabling his horse, he gave the stable boy coins and instructions on when he'd return, then headed to the Thistle Down Inn a short distance away.

A bell in the church's tower tolled the hour, reminding the townspeople it was time for Sunday mass. There was what amounted to a small army surrounding the church, as though it protected a vast treasure.

He kept his head down as he headed toward the inn on the corner. According to the date over the door, the inn had opened for business around the turn of the thirteenth century. If Fiona was correct, the door was inside. One time-travel jump, and he'd reach twenty-first century Glastonbury, then another jump in Glastonbury would take him to the Matchmaker Café in Washington State. The journey was like taking connecting flights, only there weren't layovers or missed planes involved, just thundering headaches.

He entered the inn and paused as his eyes adjusted to the low light. A fireplace doled out a pitiful amount of warmth, and candles dripped tallow onto wood tables. A few patrons sat at tables, drinking their ale in silence, ignoring the call to church. The atmosphere held the weight of despair. In this century, the only reason people came here on a Sunday was that they weren't welcome anywhere else.

Liam walked through the inn until he reached a back storeroom. Barrels of potatoes were stacked against the far wall, and cured hams hung from the ceiling. On his left was a door with a Scottish Thistle carved into the wood. The door was locked.

He glanced over his shoulder to make sure he wasn't being watched, took out his key, turned the lock, opened the door, and stepped over a mist-shrouded threshold.

Chapter Nine

Present Day

Liam had arrived at the Matchmaker Café from Glastonbury late last night, and from the look of their suitcases, had caught Bridget and Lady Roselyn just in time. He hadn't had time to change or take a shower, and suspected he smelled like wet goat. He'd debriefed the matchmaker sisters on Merlin's Curse and Colin. Lady Roselyn was taking longer than usual to decide what to do, and the longer he waited the more he worried. There was no guarantee she would agree to help find a match for the young lord.

The sisters had transformed the café into a winter wonderland reminiscent of the Regency era. The pine tree was decorated with red, green, and gold hand-blown glass ornaments, and the lights were shaped like lit candles. Boughs of cedar were draped over the fireplace mantel and framed the doors. It was still too early for customers, so he had the place to himself.

Lady Roselyn had wanted to know why Fiona had stayed behind, and Bridget wanted to know what cities they'd visited on their honeymoon. When he explained the circumstances to the sisters, they didn't look pleased and had left the room.

What he and Fiona were asking was unorthodox. To his knowledge, the sisters had never been involved in trying to break a curse, let alone bringing someone forward in time. Until now, they had only sent couples back. Now that Liam had returned to the twenty-first century, with electricity, running water, and scientific reasoning, the whole thing seemed absurd.

Had he and Fiona been caught up in the Merlin's Curse scenario because of the castle's connection to King Arthur? There was probably a logical explanation to why the wives died in childbirth that had more to do with the times in which they lived and less with a curse. No wonder the sisters looked at him as though he'd sprouted wings like the ones Fiona suspected her half-sister Nessa had.

He finished off the tea Bridget had poured into a ridiculously small china cup with tiny blue flowers, wishing he'd thought ahead and asked for a giant mug of coffee. He needed more caffeine. More importantly, he needed to return to Fiona. He didn't like that she was alone.

Thinking he'd make a pot of coffee, he rose and headed in the direction of the kitchen. Lady Roselyn and Bridget took that moment to reappear, blocking his path. Nessa was nowhere in sight. Of course, that wasn't so unusual. She often appeared and disappeared without warning.

Lady Roselyn tucked her hands into the sleeves of her jacket, like a nun preparing to quote scripture. "You and Fiona are too late. Nessa matched Colin last year, and it appears he left quite an impression on the woman. Your being here tells me that we have to reach Madeline in time. I fear that either your wife or Nessa will try to get these two people together again. And until we know more about how to break the curse, I can't allow that to happen. We leave for Glastonbury right away."

Chapter Ten

Madeline jolted awake in the back of a black limo that drove a hair below the speed limit along the British highway toward Glastonbury, England. Her mother had arranged for a limo, with a driver named William, to pick her up at the London airport. The British countryside rolled past her in a muddy brown blur as sheets of rain splashed against her window. Time-wise, it was a little after noon but felt like it should be closer to sunset. Gray fog clung to the ground and crawled up stone fences and surrounded trees as bare boned as skeletons. A dismal time of year for a wedding. No wonder most brides chose the spring and summer months to wed. When she married, she'd choose…

"Stop it," she said aloud, sitting up straighter. "You're never getting married."

"Is everything all right, lass?" The driver asked in a thick Scottish accent.

She reached for her purse, searching for a brush and mirror and maybe an attitude readjustment. She hadn't seen her mother yet, and already her thoughts had turned to forgotten dreams. "Yes, thank you, William. I didn't get a chance to sleep on the plane. I had a lot of work."

"'Tis good, then, that we are almost there. This be the season for celebration, romance, and possibilities, not stress and deadlines. Your mother was well pleased when she received your message. Her husband-to-be said your mother wouldn't go through with their wedding if her only child couldn't be there to give her away."

Madeline felt a pang of guilt. Had her mother believed she wouldn't come to the wedding? It was true that, over the past year, Madeline hadn't seen her mother or Gran more than a few times. She'd been busy. Her job didn't afford her a lot of free time.

The driver glanced in his rearview mirror at her as though expecting a response.

Madeline nodded; hoping agreement would silence him as she met the glance. He reminded her of Sean Connery in his later years, wearing a wool tweed cap over salt-and-pepper hair. There had been a hint of judgment in his voice, which caused her to break the connection and resume her examination of the countryside. If the driver was judging her, he'd have to get in line.

The limo skirted the town of Glastonbury and headed down a narrow street lined with shrubs. "This is a beautiful town," she said to the driver.

"Did you know that Glastonbury is believed by some to be one of the sites of Camelot and Arthur's Knights of the Round Table? Others believe it was the Isle of Avalon."

She did know Glastonbury's connection to the Arthurian legends, because that was all her mother and Gran had ever talked about since Madeline could remember.

And their passion had become hers. She'd stopped attending fairs when she went off to college and then law school. Last year's Christmas Eve party was the first time she'd worn a costume in years, and the experience with Colin made her wonder if maybe it was time for a new passion. Time to put away such fantasies. Magical kingdoms and chivalrous knights no longer existed.

The limo rolled to a stop, and the driver jumped out to open the door.

The moment she stepped out of the limo, her mother was waiting outside as though William had called ahead.

"You're here." Her mother's bracelets jangled together as she wrapped Madeline in a warm embrace.

Madeline had forgotten that her mother always smelled like lavender and cloves and had a smile that brought sunshine to the gloomiest day. She shut her eyes to push back a tear and returned the embrace. She had missed those smells and images. She'd missed her mother.

"Where's Gran?"

"Here I am, my darling girl." Gran waved from the porch steps and walked to Madeline straight and tall and without a limp. She looked ten years younger, as though the English air agreed with her. The last time Madeline had seen Gran was four months ago. She paused. No, make that eight. She cringed. That was awful. She'd have to do better.

She ran to Gran and hugged her. "I missed you. I missed you both."

Her mother came alongside Madeline and Gran. "We missed you more than you can imagine, and I'm so glad you were able to catch an earlier flight. Our first party is this evening. You'll have a chance for a nap and a quick bite before it starts. Oh, I almost forgot."

She handed Madeline an envelope. "It arrived late last night from Lady Roselyn. I hope it's good news."

Chapter Eleven

The news from Lady Roselyn not only wasn't good, it was confusing. She'd said that she hadn't found Colin and under no circumstances was Madeline to allow Nessa to walk her over a threshold. Okay, so that made no sense.

What *was* good news was her room. It looked like an exhibit from a museum. There was a four-poster bed with dragons carved into the wood, red velvet drapes and coverlet, edged in gold, and walls covered in tapestries.

Her mother opened the drapes, bringing in more light, but the day was still gray, and soon even that miserly light would be extinguished by the night. "Everything you'll need is in the wardrobe closet. I've asked all of our guests to remain in period costume for the duration of their stay." Her mother faced the window, turning only her head toward Madeline. "I know your father asked you to try and persuade me to sign over my shares to him. Failure is not something your father likes to admit. Were you aware that he's getting another divorce?"

"I wasn't, but I can't say I'm surprised," Madeline said, remembering her father's rejected expression. She opened her briefcase and removed the folder holding the contract as well as work from her office. "I think Father is still in love with you."

Her mother lowered her head. "A part of me will always love him as well. The question of whether or not we loved each other was never the issue between us. It was acceptance." Her mother pressed her forehead against a pane of glass, her shoulders shaking.

Madeline didn't know what to say. Her mother had never been so candid about her relationship with Madeline's father before. "I'm sorry…"

Her mother straightened, swiping at her face as she turned. "If it's all right with you, I'd like to wait until after the wedding to review the contract. You have officially entered a work-free zone. There is a ball tonight to kick off the celebrations, one that is even more grand than the one I planned last Christmas Eve." She crossed over to the bed and, taking the folder from Madeline's hands, deposited it into the briefcase. Her eyes widened as she withdrew a book. "You brought the gift I gave you last Christmas, *The Death of Arthur.*"

Madeline reached for the book bound to look like the original, with a leather-like cover and old-world script on sepia-toned paper. "That's funny. I don't remember packing it in my briefcase."

Her mother put her arm around Madeline's shoulder. "I'm glad you did. When I bought it for you last year, it reminded me of how much you used to love going to the reenactment fairs. Remember the time when you borrowed a helmet and tried to sneak onto the jousting field to challenge the White Knight?"

Madeline traced her fingers over the embossed sword on the cover that reminded her of the one made out of wood that she'd used at the fair. "I would have succeeded, too, if someone hadn't stopped me."

Her mother closed and locked the briefcase. "Well, you were only twelve at the time."

Madeline opened the book to the title page, where her mother had written, *To Madeline, my little warrior. Never give up on your dreams.*

At the fair, surrounded by a dozen officials, her mother had been the warrior, arguing her case that there was no mention of an age or gender restriction when it came to challenging the White Knight to mock combat. It was at that moment Madeline decided she wanted to be a lawyer like her mother.

Madeline gripped the book against her chest. "I don't think I ever thanked you for arguing in my defense."

Her mother laughed. "You're welcome, and the only reason you weren't allowed to challenge the White Knight is that those silly men realized they were losing the argument and closed the event." Her mother winked. "They thought you might beat the White Knight."

Madeline swept her mother into a hug. "I'm glad I'm here."

"Me too. I forgot to ask. When can we expect Colin to arrive?"

Madeline covered the note Lady Roselyn had sent her and slid it toward her mother, reviewing the excuses she could use. She mentally eliminated all of them. No more lies. "He's not coming. That was what the note from Lady Roselyn was about. Colin and I aren't dating. In fact, the first and only time I met him was at the Christmas Eve party a year ago. A matchmaker arranged the whole thing. A few weeks ago, I asked Lady Roselyn if she could find him again, but her note said he had all but disappeared into thin air. I'm sorry. I know you and Gran thought I was dating this fabulous guy."

"Honey, I'm your mother. I knew the moment I saw you and Colin together that you were meeting him for the first time. The two of you were so fun to watch. There were so many sparks it was a wonder the room didn't burst into flames."

"That's not true. There weren't sparks. I admit he was sort of good-looking, and he did save Gran. He's just…I mean…he's…"

"Gorgeous and chivalrous are the words you're looking for," her mother said.

"It doesn't matter. He's not coming."

Chapter Twelve

Tintagel Castle—Fifteenth Century

Avoiding the Great Hall, Colin spotted his friend, Douglas Channing, in a sitting area with high ceilings. Douglas's father had been one of Lord Penrose's trusted commanders and had died saving the lord's life. Stocky and broad-chested like his father, Douglas was a trusted member of the family.

Douglas stepped aside, exposing that he was engaged in a hushed conversation with the Lady Dorothy. Colin hesitated, concerned he was interrupting. While he debated joining them, the Lady Dorothy bid goodbye to Douglas and nodded a silent acknowledgement to Colin as she glided past him into the Great Hall. Her silence was unusual, but then he'd interrupted a private conversation. Was this the woman Douglas had mentioned a few months ago he wanted to marry? If so, Colin was pleased.

Douglas had few friends, and of late Colin worried that his friend spent more and more time alone. Colin grimaced. The same thing had been said about him.

He and Douglas had drifted in different directions recently. Douglas longed for a family of his own, while Colin searched for a solution to Merlin's Curse. He envied his friend. The man could marry for love.

Douglas greeted Colin, clasping his arm. "How is

your father today? I will plan to visit him this afternoon after he's rested."

"My father believes he is dying and threatens that if I do not wed, he will declare my cousin Henry Blackstone his heir."

Douglas sucked in his breath. "Your father sounds serious this time. But I have faith he will recover. Your father is strong."

Colin shook his head. "He is not the man he once was. He looks fragile. I am not sure if it was the result of his injuries or that I never wanted to notice the changes in him as he grew older. He has lost the spark in his eyes, as though he is letting go of this world and longs for the next, the world where he will see my mother again." Colin scrubbed his hand over his face. "Let us talk of happier things. Is the Lady Dorothy the fair woman you spoke of to me before I left for Dozmary Pool?"

Douglas massaged his left arm. He had broken the arm in a fall years ago while he and Colin had been climbing trees. The arm had healed, but Douglas still rubbed it when he was anxious or afraid. "I have asked the Lady Dorothy to marry me, and she promises she will consider my proposal offer."

His friend did not have a taste for battle, and Colin was grateful he was here to watch over his father and their lands. It would also mean the Lady Dorothy would not have to worry about her husband dying on the battlefield, yet he noted the hesitation and fear in Douglas's voice. Wanting to encourage him, he said, "You are a fine man, and the lady will recognize your worth."

Douglas slipped his hands into the folds of his

tunic, his expression guarded. "Your father said the same. But I harbor no illusions. I am a man without a title."

The entrance doors opened, ushering in icy winds and five members of the clergy. Hooded robes spiraled around their bodies until the doors closed behind them, but their faces remained cloaked in the shadows of their hoods. Each man nodded in turn toward Colin, acknowledging his status as Lord Penrose's son.

"Those are priests from Father Patrick Blackstone's parish in Glastonbury," Colin said, "and are little more than witch hunters in priests' clothing. There was a time when they were not welcome. What are they doing here?"

"Your father asked Father Patrick to preside over your wedding, and knowing you do not look on him kindly, Father Patrick insisted the priests should precede him here."

Colin swore under his breath. "He and his priests prey on the weak and the innocent. Of course I do not look upon him *kindly*. In addition, he is Henry's brother. If I fail to marry, he will demand my father name his brother as heir."

"A good assessment of the situation. Since your father's accident, he has grown more anxious. It is good that you came back when you did, then. Last week he vowed to declare me his heir if you did not return from your quest by Christmas Eve. He believes Father Patrick's lies that Excalibur is a tale told by witches to corrupt the innocent and that nothing will lift Merlin's Curse."

Colin hesitated, not doubting he could trust Douglas with the news that he had planned to renew his search for Excalibur in a new location, but concerned someone would overhear their conversation. Every castle and manor house had its spies, ready to share secrets, and Castle Tintagel was no exception. He chose a safer topic.

"My father suggested I employ a matchmaker to find a bride willing to marry me."

Douglas did not seem as surprised as Colin would have thought. "The matchmaker Fiona is here with her husband on holiday," he said soberly. "Your father mentioned he might ask her. Did Fiona agree?"

Colin nodded. "My father does not ask. He orders. I am to meet her in the chapel."

Douglas shook his head slowly. "The matchmaker is either a great fool or an eternal romantic to believe she can convince a woman to risk her life to love a Penrose."

Chapter Thirteen

The chapel was decorated for the season with boughs of fir and holly, their red berries in contrast to the shine of the green leaves. Colin had entered the chapel a short time ago, searching for peace and clarity. Was Douglas right? Even if Colin could break the curse, would any woman want to take the risk by marrying him?

His mother had married his father knowing the risk, and their courtship and love had inspired minstrels. This was the only time of year the chapel looked festive, his father's way of honoring the death of his mother. He could do the same. He could build a shrine in memory of a wife who bore his child. A grisly thought.

He rubbed his eyes with the palm of his hands and moved to stand beneath the words of Merlin's Curse, etched on a granite tablet and bolted to the chapel's pillar next to the altar. He knew it by heart.

For the sin of stealing my love,

I, Merlin, Wizard, Wise Man, and teacher of Arthur, the one true king, place this curse upon the Penrose Clan.

Return what is stolen to its rightful resting place.

Until then, women will die giving birth to a Penrose heir.

Only a woman out of time holds the key to

unlocking this curse.

The matchmaker Fiona had arrived a short time ago and stood reading and re-reading Merlin's words. Like her sister Nessa, Fiona had been confident she and her sisters could find Colin a match. What she would not guarantee was if the woman would agree to marry him or if the curse could be broken. She needed more information.

"Tell me what you know about Merlin's Curse."

"Merlin's Curse condemns a Penrose wife to certain death within hours of giving birth. Our vanity fuels the belief that the cost of continuing our line is more important than the lives it costs. It is time the curse died with me."

She shivered, rubbing her arms. "Harsh. You are to be commended that you don't want to marry unless you can break the curse. Your father, though, is rather insistent."

"He believes the cost is worth it."

"Then our task is to break the curse. What else do you know?"

"In books and letters I have read on the subject, Merlin talks about someone stealing his great love. The most accepted opinion is that the great love he mentions is Nimue, the woman he loved and kept safe when he turned her into a tree," Colin said.

"You believe it's something else," Fiona said.

"You are perceptive."

"It's part of being a matchmaker, and I've also read a lot about curses. There are always hidden meanings and clues."

"I believe the love Merlin was talking about was Excalibur. According to legend, after the death of

Arthur, Excalibur was returned to the Lady of the Lake, who legend claims lives in Dozmary Pool. Many have searched over the centuries, but the pool hides her secrets well. What is not widely known is that one of my ancestors found the sword and gave it to the Church in Glastonbury in atonement for the atrocities he committed during his life. The bishop of Glastonbury, moved by the generosity, assured the man that God would forgive him all his sins, and he hid the sword," said Colin.

"It's rumored around the castle that you have been searching for Excalibur for almost ten years."

Colin pushed away from the pillar. How much should he tell Fiona? He had no reason to trust her. They had just met. Her claim that she was a matchmaker and that she was confident she could find him a bride could be just words. There was no proof she would succeed. But he was no closer to finding Excalibur than he had been when he began his quest. He had asked his cousin Henry if there was any truth to the rumor regarding the Glastonbury legend. Colin had received a resounding no. Henry had explained that if there had been a sword of such value, he would have heard about it, as his brother, the parish priest, would have found and sold it.

Colin folded his arms across his chest. "The rumors of my search for Arthur's sword are true, but of late I fear it is like the search for the Holy Grail."

Fiona reread Merlin's words. "In essence, what you are saying is that Excalibur may be unattainable. The fact that you believe it is real suggests that you also believe Merlin was a wizard and Camelot was real."

He narrowed his gaze. Was the woman deliberately

provoking him? "How could I not believe in such things? Or do you think it a coincidence that since Merlin first penned his curse, no woman has survived giving birth to a Penrose child?"

"I don't believe in coincidences."

"Neither do I."

She hesitated. "Then you believe in enchantments, magic, and things not easily explained? For example, it is said that, among other things, Merlin could control time."

"You are speaking of witchcraft and sorcery."

Her expression froze as she waited for his answer. "And if I were?"

He turned to face the plaque. "I do not know whether I do or not. All I know is that my mother died giving me life, and I refuse to allow one more Penrose child to grow up without a mother. If that means asking a witch to save our family, so be it."

She let out a sigh, as though she had been holding her breath. "Good. Now, instead of Excalibur, we will concentrate on finding you a woman out of time. Maybe that alone will satisfy the conditions of the curse. I believe I know what 'out of time' means. How far are you willing to go for a bride?"

"To the ends of the earth. Even if you succeed, and this woman agrees to marry me, how will we know if the curse has been lifted?"

"Good question. My guess is that the plaque will crack in two."

He followed her gaze. "Are you sure?"

"Not at all."

Chapter Fourteen

Present Day

The euphoria Madeline had felt visiting with Gran and her mother faded into the shadows of the Thistle Down Inn in Glastonbury. She felt the walls close in around her as she headed toward the first of many parties leading to her mother's wedding. The inn was too warm and the Christmas music too loud. Everyone she met offered to set her up with a date for her mother's wedding.

Her head spun with the building of a storm-sized headache. She caught sight of her mother's friends. They'd want to ask her about her relationship status, show her pictures of grandkids, then offer their sad faces when she confessed she was single, a fate worse than death in her parents' circles.

"Over here," Nessa signaled, motioning for Madeline to join her by an alcove.

Madeline rushed over. "What are you doing here? Lady Roselyn said she planned to come, but I didn't realize it would be this soon."

Nessa looked toward the entrance as though Lady Roselyn might appear at any moment. "Lady Roselyn is coming? When did she say she'd arrive?"

"Her note said late tonight or tomorrow morning, depending on flights."

Nessa took both Madeline's hands in hers. "Then we don't have much time. Do you still want to see Colin again?"

"Lady Roselyn said she couldn't find him."

Nessa frowned. "That's because she isn't sure where to look. You didn't answer my question. Do you want to see Colin again?"

"I'm not sure."

"Fair enough. When you are sure, I'll be here waiting. After Lady Roselyn arrives, however, it will be too late. She will try to stop me from sending you to the fifteenth century."

Chapter Fifteen

Twinkling lights were strung over the entrance of the restaurant in the Thistle Down Inn and a Christmas tree placed in its center, lending the illusion that the party took place outside under a canopy of stars. Boughs of fir and holly draped over the mantel of the gas-and-electric fireplace as Madeline inhaled the forest smells, smiling. Her mother had hung sprigs of mistletoe, knowing that during the Dark Ages it was forbidden by the Church because of its pagan symbol of fertility.

That was so much like her mother. She was outspoken on the Church's suppression of women and its narrow-minded view on things it didn't understand. She was glad she'd come.

Like herself, the guests were dressed in medieval costumes and having a good time. After the conservative suits she wore at her office, the loose-fitting dress was a welcome change. It made her feel like a kid again, attending reenactment fairs with her mother or dressing up for Halloween.

Her conversation with the matchmaker, Nessa, after her mother had gone for a dress fitting, kept replaying in her mind at an increasing rate. Nessa had proposed that Madeline could travel to the Middle Ages and pick out a date for her mother's wedding as though she were shopping for a dress or a pair of shoes.

Why go to such extremes as to make up a story about time travel? Madeline guessed that the matchmaker would spirit her away to some elaborate reenactment fair, like the one in Fall City, Washington. But what if Nessa's claim was true?

She laughed softly. She actually was thinking time travel was possible. She blamed the dress she was wearing. As a child she'd dreamed of living in the Middle Ages, and she knew her mother had as well. Her mother had gone to a lot of trouble to create a Camelot-themed wedding, and even if there were no such thing as time travel, her mother's gift to her guests was that they could pretend.

The downside was that Madeline knew her father had invited her ex-boyfriend.

Timothy was in the crowd, shaking hands and pretending he loved everything. Most people would believe him and find him charming. That was one of his strengths. The other was that he was one of the most beautiful men she'd ever met, the kind of man who could make the cover of *People Magazine*'s Most Attractive Man of the Year issue.

"There you are." Timothy held out his hand toward her, pulling her into the restaurant. A small gesture, like an olive branch, representing an apology and the hope for a new beginning.

It would be so easy to slip back into the life they'd lived before she'd walked in on him and the law firm's intern, naked and having sex in her bed. She shuddered, trying to erase the memory that had been seared into her brain. "Here I am," she said, tightening her jaw.

"You look wonderful." He leaned down until their faces were so close she could see the shades of amber in his eyes—eyes that lied.

She kept her voice cordial, as though she were talking to a client. "My father said you're up for partner."

His smile widened. It had been his smile that had first attracted her attention. It accentuated his chiseled jaw, his cheekbones, and his crazy good looks. Back then, she'd believed that if a person had a great smile, it was a positive sign.

"All business as usual," he said. "Yes, my promotion looks promising. What about you? Have you changed your mind about making partner?"

"I don't want to discuss it." Becoming partner had come with a long list of conditions. The types of cases and clients she would represent, followed by the image she must present, which in her father's opinion meant she was married, but the most distasteful was that he'd wanted her to give up her *pro bono* work as a defense attorney in exchange for working with the firm's clients when they had personal issues.

He turned her to face him and gestured to the sprig of mistletoe hanging over their heads. "A kiss for old times' sake?" His breath caressed her skin, his voice seductive like a spider, pulling her into its web.

Her body tensed. Her first impulse was to slap the grin off his face. But a kiss was a small thing, wasn't it? She didn't want to make a scene. People were in the restaurant taking pictures, laughing, having a good time. Then the image of him and Barbara in bed together flashed into her mind again, and what he'd said screamed in her head.

She drew back and balled her fists at her sides. "Why are you here?"

"You're still upset. I see that. The affair was a moment of weakness."

"Seriously? Your moment of weakness had been going on for six months, which was the same length of time we'd been dating."

He brushed a long strand of her hair behind her ear. "I was an idiot."

She remembered that he liked her long hair neat and pulled back, or piled on top of her head. She jerked her curls back down onto her face. She would not get drawn into his web again. "What is this really about? Did my father give you the same ultimatum he gave me? You can't make partner unless you are married or engaged? You know he can't enforce that outdated rule."

Timothy's expression hardened, marring his good looks. "No, the Board can't legally enforce your father's outdated morality. They can, however, make it difficult."

"And you like things easy."

The muscles along his jawline hardened "Why are you being so stubborn? If we marry, we both get what we want."

Madeline shook her head, backing away from him. "I don't know what I want. I need more time."

He snorted. "Time has always been your problem. You overthink everything and take too much time to make a decision."

"I prefer to look at all angles. That's what makes me a good lawyer."

"Life isn't like a courtroom." He spread his arms to encompass the ballroom and the crowd gathered for her mother's wedding reception. "Nor is it like this fantasy your mother created. She's filled you with the idea unselfish love exists. It's like the illusion she's created for her wedding reception. Love isn't real, and men aren't like those at the fairs you and she used to attend. They don't rescue damsels in distress without expecting something in return."

"You're wrong."

He shoved his hands into his pockets and looked toward the ballroom. "Your mother made it clear that you needed a date for her wedding. A not-so-subtle way of saying that she wants you married, or at least in a relationship that has a future. All I'm asking is that you give us a second chance."

When he said it, he made it sound so simple. She'd accused him of liking things easy. The truth was that so did she, when it came to relationships. She hated drama. She had enough of it practicing law. She didn't believe for a minute that he wouldn't cheat again. But would it really matter? She'd make partner.

But Timothy didn't want children. He'd made that clear on more than one occasion. She'd pushed having children onto the back burner while building her career. With Timothy, there wouldn't be children.

A life without children flashed like the trailer of a movie. She'd never hold a child of her own, play with her, or help him with homework. Her mother wouldn't have the chance to dress up her grandchildren in silly medieval costumes and tell stories that made history come alive.

She wanted all of that. She wanted children. Her breath caught in her throat. What was she thinking?

"It was nice to see you, Timothy," she said, holding out her hand to shake his one more time. It had been nice. She now had clarity. "I already have a date. Or I will."

Timothy's mouth gaped open. Not a good look. She chuckled, picked up her skirts, and raced up the stairs, hoping Nessa was still there.

Chapter Sixteen

This was really happening. Madeline felt like a child who just learned that her parents were taking her to the most famous amusement park in the world. But like a roller coaster ride, her emotions were all over the place. She felt excited, apprehensive, and—God help her—turned on at the prospect of seeing Colin again.

With Nessa leading the way, they continued down a series of corridors to a place in the inn that looked older than the rest of the house. A few of the windows were little more than long, narrow slits, while others were covered over with window shutters. At last, Nessa paused at a door with the image of a Scottish thistle burned into the wood and the number 1485 painted above.

"I know that date," Madeline said. "It was the year Malory's book *The Death of Arthur* was published."

"Then you will really like what's behind this door," Nessa said.

"Does it lead outside?" Madeline ventured, peering out a window to get her bearings. The starless night and absence of streetlights didn't help. She felt turned around, not sure if she was at the front or back of the house.

"Like all of our enchanted doors, this one opens to new possibilities. You mentioned that you wanted to see Colin again."

Madeline eyed the door. "Enchanted? What are you saying…exactly?"

Nessa winked. "What if I told you that when you walk over this threshold, you'll enter another time in history?"

"You're talking about time travel?" Madeline stepped back.

Nessa didn't look crazy. But then neither did some of her father's clients. Looks could be deceiving. That was the first lesson she'd learned at the firm—that, and how to avoid being alone with unstable clients. Madeline pointed over her shoulder in the direction of the staircase at the end of the hallway. "I should go back."

"You don't believe me."

Madeline let out a clipped laugh. "You are one hundred percent correct. I don't believe you. You're talking about time travel."

Nessa's eyes sparkled with mischief as she nodded. "What if I am?"

"Okay…yes, I would like to see Colin again. My mother and Gran like him, and it's no wonder, if what you say is true and he's a real-life knight. I could invite him as my date to my mother's wedding. If it didn't work out between us, the best part would be that I could return him, like a Christmas present that didn't fit. I would tell my parents that we were engaged…" Madeline shook her head. "What am I thinking? Fantasies aren't real, and wishes and dreams don't come true. I'm expected downstairs."

"Fantasies are real, and wishes and dreams come true every day. You just have to believe."

She'd dreamed of visiting the mythical time of

King Arthur and his Knights of the Round Table. She'd never imagined the dream would come true. How could she? Time travel only happened in make-believe stories.

Nessa fastened a gold locket, etched with a Scottish thistle, around Madeline's neck. "The locket will identify you in case we are separated. My sister Fiona will be at Tintagel Castle."

Madeline fingered the pendant, trying to ground her emotions. "What do you mean, 'if we get separated'?"

"You have nothing to worry about. We are skilled matchmakers, and we have everything under control. There were a few glitches with some of our past adventures, but that has been handled. What you are about to witness is not a reenactment. Once you step over the threshold, you will enter the fifteenth century. I will be going with you, and as soon as we arrive, we'll hire a coach and connect with Fiona at Tintagel Castle. Now, this is very important—it's critical that you tell no one you are from the future. In this century, women are burned or hanged as witches for a rebellious word, or even for healing a sick person when others failed to cure them. Traveling through time will seem like the Devil's work. Are you one hundred percent sure you wish to take this leap?"

"Well, not now!"

Nessa arched a brow. "Have you changed your mind?"

"I'm kidding. I think. Will it hurt?"

Nessa shook her head as she unlocked the door. "It affects people in different ways. I find it invigorating, while my sisters like to take a nap afterwards. Reactions can be all over the map. But there is no pain."

Mist the shade of wet steel, fused with diamond-like points of light, swirled toward Madeline's feet as though beckoning her to cross the threshold. It spread over her cloth shoes and moved to blanket the hallway's timeworn ruby-red carpet until it confronted the door on the opposite side.

The thrill that had spread over her skin with the appearance of the mist intensified. "How long will we stay?"

Madeline adjusted the embroidered gold-braid belt that slung loosely around her waist, bringing out the gold threads in her forest-green gown. Nessa had assured her that her gown, with its bell sleeves and figure-hugging lines, was appropriate for the time period. She laughed nervously. What she was about to do seemed surreal. Maybe this was a mistake.

Nessa glanced at the time on the grandfather clock in the hallway and frowned. "My sister has arrived. You have to leave now." Nessa appeared distracted, fidgeting with the key that had unlocked the door.

"Is everything all right? Should we wait for Lady Roselyn?"

Nessa's forehead furrowed as she tapped her fingers on the doorknob. "Usually it takes three matchmaker sisters for the time travel enchantment to work properly. I found a loophole. When you meet Colin, make sure he tells you about the curse. I planned to, but there isn't time."

"Curse? Did you say curse?"

The grandfather clock against the wall chimed its countdown to midnight.

Female voices, raised in argument, echoed from the

staircase at the end of the hallway.

Nessa flinched. "Lady Roselyn is here. You have to go now. Are you ready?"

Madeline recognized the panic in Nessa's voice. Something was wrong. Then she remembered the confusing note Lady Roselyn had sent. It had told her not to let Nessa walk her over a threshold. "Should we wait for your sister?"

Lady Roselyn appeared down the hall, wearing an expression as dark as her suit. "Stop!"

In the next instant, Nessa pushed Madeline over the threshold and slammed the door shut behind her.

Chapter Seventeen

Fifteenth Century

A drafty hearth coughed out a smoky haze that hung over the Thistle Down Inn's tavern.

Candles sputtered and dripped tallow onto food-stained wooden tables. Alcohol-fueled laughter smothered conversations as Henry Blackstone the Fourth finished his tankard of ale, with instructions to bring another. He was not drunk enough yet.

His spies at Tintagel Castle had informed him that Lord Penrose had hired a matchmaker to find his son a bride in time for the Christmas Eve celebration. Henry had spent vast sums of money spreading reminders of the consequences of Merlin's Curse across the kingdom, warning what befell Penrose wives and mistresses who gave birth to a Penrose heir. His campaign had reaped his objective. Women and their families treated Colin as though he had leprosy. None wanted to sacrifice themselves or their daughters to certain death. He had not counted on a matchmaker, especially one who his informant at Tintagel claimed had solved the meaning of the line in the curse, "a woman out of time."

Getting his hands on the Penrose fortune seemed more remote than ever, and he needed the money to repair his debts before his father found out and disowned him. Without his father's support, Henry would be thrown into debtor's prison.

He looked up, searching for the woman who'd served him. He was starting to sober.

A tankard slapped down in front of him as a priest pulled up a bench at Henry's table and deposited a parcel on the spare bench. "You looked thirsty."

Henry thanked his younger brother and downed half the contents. Even with common parents and only two years separating them in age, they looked nothing alike, save for their ghost-gray eyes. Patrick was weasel-thin, whereas Henry had the broad shoulders of a warrior, or so his mother had boasted with pride, only to have been corrected by his father, who had announced that Henry would grow into a tavern brawler.

"What are you doing here, Patrick? If you're looking for money, I intend to spend the last of the coin in my purse on getting drunk."

"From the look of you I'd say you are already well on your way. And it's *Father* Patrick Blackstone to you." His brother's voice spilled out in a hiss through the space between his front teeth. "Show respect for a man of the cloth."

"Save your speech for your congregation. I know the secrets you hide and the reason our father forced you into the priesthood. Again, why are you here?"

Father Patrick's eyes narrowed into dark slits. "Information. Is it true that a matchmaker was hired to find Colin a bride? Must I remind you of our agreement? I help you become the Penrose heir, and in return, you spend a portion of the Penroses' vast fortune to enlarge my church. That will gain me recognition in

Rome and likely make me a bishop or a cardinal."

Henry finished his ale and hailed for another. "You aim high. I am surprised, though, that your ambitions do not rise higher. Why not Pope Patrick?"

"The Italians own the papacy," Father Patrick said with a sneer. "This is a setback. My source tells me that the matchmaker told Colin she would arrange for him to meet a woman here at the inn. According to Penrose laws, our cousin must marry by age thirty, and produce an heir from that union within a year, or forfeit his inheritance. Colin turns thirty on Christmas Eve. Time is running out for him, and yet he has made it clear that he will not risk a woman's life as long as the curse still holds power over his family. The man is a fool. If we prevent Colin from meeting this woman, Colin's father will be forced to declare you his heir."

"Some would say that Colin is a hero," Henry said, "for caring more for a woman's life than for wealth and power."

"It will be well if you do not succumb to the same weakness of consequence when you become the heir."

Henry focused his blurred vision on the amber liquid in his tankard. Could he be as callous as his brother suggested?

"Colin arrives tonight with the matchmaker," Patrick confirmed. "We must prevent him from meeting with whomever the matchmaker has selected for him."

"Do you know what the woman looks like?"

"All I know is that they are meeting at the inn, which is why I asked you to meet me here."

"Not the only reason," Henry said, tilting his head to include the parcel on the bench beside him. "What church relic are you selling tonight?"

"Lower your voice. The man has not yet arrived."

"One day, brother, your greed will be your undoing. Exactly why am I here?"

Father Patrick leaned in closer. "I am concerned for your cousin. In his desperation, he has aligned himself with a witch, for how else would you describe a matchmaker who claims she can find a bride with the power to break a curse? Only God has power over the dark arts."

Henry swallowed a belch, leaning against the wall. He rubbed his hand over his eyes. "My brain is not so fogged with drink that I believe you care for Colin's immortal soul. This is about the woman. As for witchcraft, you are not a stranger to the dark arts."

Patrick glanced over his shoulder. "Take care in what you say. The Church condemns what it cannot understand and eliminates any threat to its power."

Henry finished his ale and set it aside. "You and the Church share a common philosophy. Again…what has this to do with me?"

Father Patrick shook his head, his lips a thin angry line. "I believe the woman will arrive tonight. We must check if there is word of her arrival, intercept her, and prevent her and Colin from meeting. Stay vigilant. I will return soon."

Patrick left the table to join a group of men at the far corner of the tavern, and Henry stared after him. His brother had just told him to kill someone, as dispassionately as if he were asking for another round of drinks. Until this moment, Henry hadn't known how far Patrick had fallen. The question for Henry was if he could wallow in the same cesspool as his brother.

****

Another tankard of foaming ale appeared on Henry's table, compliments of Father Patrick.

Henry waved acknowledgment to his brother, who was sequestered with the group of men on the other side of the tavern. They looked like the traveling bands of Romani who made this area their home and stole a person blind. If not for the protection of Colin and his father, the Romani would be in jail, or hanged. When he was heir, he'd make sure they got what they deserved.

Henry fought the temptation to drain the ale in one gulp and give in to the sweet release that would dull his conscience. He knew what his brother was suggesting. He wanted the woman dead. Their father had believed the priesthood would redeem Patrick. It had only fed his dark side.

Henry wasn't the only one who had accumulated gambling debts. In Patrick's case, he had sold church gold and relics and was being blackmailed to keep the crime a secret. Tonight Patrick was meeting with someone to sell another church relic. Curiosity drew Henry to the package.

Long and narrow, the package was wrapped in black velvet cloth and secured with leather thongs. Henry was working to unfasten the bindings when his brother returned.

"That belongs to me, big brother," Patrick said, returning with two men who looked as though they'd been living in the sewers. Both had the haunted look of men who'd given up on their dreams. One of his brother's talents was sensing a person's weakness and turning it to his advantage. His brother sent the men away with the order to fortify their courage at the bar as he joined Henry, nodding to the entrance of the inn.

"A woman arrived a short time ago, one the innkeeper can't identify. She appeared in the upstairs hallway as though by sorcery. She must be the one mentioned by the matchmaker."

Henry followed Patrick's gaze. After the red hair, the next thing Henry noticed was the expression in the woman's eyes. It reminded him of how his sister had looked the day he'd taken her to Glastonbury's May Day festival. His sister had been excited and curious about everything, especially the colorful travelers from the East who told fortunes and performed magic tricks, and about the unfamiliar aromas of curry and saffron that wafted from their food booths, and the music they made that quickened the blood.

His sister had wanted to return the next day. His parents had refused, furious that he'd taken her in the first place. They feared that his sister, who had never been in good health, would be infected by one of the many illnesses that plagued Europe.

In the end, his parents had been right. She'd died a short time later of the Black Death, and his mother soon after. Henry finished his ale and looked away. The day he buried his mother and sister was the day Henry had lost his faith.

Patrick cuffed Henry on the shoulder. "Now is your chance. Seduce her with that notorious charm of yours, and once she is in a secluded place, you must kill her."

Henry flinched. He had known that was his brother's intention. Hearing it voiced still shook him. "You want me to commit murder? You condemn my soul to hell. I am many things, but never have I killed an innocent."

"I'm a priest with the power to grant forgiveness. If Colin marries this woman, and if she is as the matchmaker claims, we lose everything. You'll be thrown into debtor's prison, and I will be defrocked and thrown into the cell next to yours. I've visited these hellholes and would choose freedom and comfort in this life, with the slim possibility that God will forgive my sins and grant me entrance into heaven in the next."

"That is not the message you preach on Sunday," Henry said evenly.

Father Patrick shrugged. "I am a realist. What is your answer? Poverty or riches?"

Henry had lost his faith: now he would lose his immortal soul. Was his brother right? Was this the only way out? Henry rose on unsteady legs. "On one condition. We do this together."

Father Patrick lurched back, his eyes blinking. "I am a priest. I cannot be seen…"

Henry settled back down and motioned for another ale.

Father Patrick flipped the hood of his robe over his head, cuffing Henry on the shoulder. "All right. Lead the way."

Henry eyed his brother. He must be desperate and in more danger of discovery than Henry had first thought. He smothered a smile. His brother wasn't the only one who'd learned from their father how to exploit a weakness. "We do this together," he repeated.

A shadow darkened Patrick's expression. "Agreed."

Henry nodded and stood, swaying. He braced himself against the table to steady his balance. Not for the first time he wished he was the type of drunk who passed out and couldn't remember what he had done the night before. Unfortunately, he remembered all his misdeeds.

He straightened his shoulders and concentrated. Fate was not on the woman's side. She headed in his direction.

"Can we be of service, milady?" Henry said, slurring his words. He cleared his throat and concentrated on speaking more clearly. "I can offer a pint of ale, perhaps, or a walk in the moonlight. My name is Henry."

Her nose wrinkled as her lips pressed together. She hesitated, then said, "My name is Madeline. Thank you for your offer, but I'm okay. I'll ask at the bar." She walked around him, heading into the heart of the tavern.

He turned with her, and in a few long strides, Henry had reached the woman's side again and placed a hand under her arm, pulling her against his side. "Are you looking for someone? I am sure I can help you."

She jerked a nod, her eyes widening in comprehension as though she smelled his intentions as clearly as she no doubt smelled the alcohol on his breath. She paused. "I'm to meet a matchmaker by the name of Fiona. Do you know her?"

Her speech pattern was clipped, and the accent unfamiliar, but the tone of her voice was pleasant enough. She seemed like a gentle person, very much like his sister—and like his sister, too young to die. Could he really murder her? If he didn't, likely his brother would find someone who would.

As though sensing his thoughts, Patrick nudged Henry in the ribs. "Do not lose your nerve," Patrick whispered.

Henry painted on the smile he'd used in the past to lure women to his bed, pulling her even closer. "I saw Fiona a short time ago. I believe she is outside. My friends and I will be honored to show you the way, milady. It is dangerous for a woman at this hour."

He could see the doubt in her eyes. The curiosity had vanished, replaced by a strong dose of apprehension. The woman had a keen intelligence, like his sister.

Her eyes widened more as she tried to wrench free of his hold. "Let me go. I'll wait for Fiona inside."

He pressed a knife to her side, covering it with the edge of his cloak, as he moved her toward the door. His brother had disappeared, but the two thugs he'd hired moved around Henry and the woman, blocking her from the view of the curious.

She screamed.

Henry was prepared.

He swept his cloak around her, covered her mouth with his hand, and whisked her outside into the cold and uncaring black of night.

A carriage lumbered into view. Laughter spilled out of it like rain as it came to a stop at the inn. The driver of the carriage jumped down from the bench seat and opened the door for the passengers. The last thing Henry needed were witnesses.

Henry dragged the woman farther into the shadows, with the two men close behind. Not surprisingly, Patrick had disappeared. Henry would deal with his brother later.

The woman struggled to free herself and fought like a cat, scratching at Henry's face and kicking his shins. The two thugs cheered her on, shouting that a woman of such spirit would be good in bed. He relaxed his grip, turning to order them to remain silent lest they be overheard.

In that split second, she kneed him in the groin, shoved Henry into the two men, and ran.

Chapter Eighteen

Colin lit the lantern in the barn and stretched. It had been a long ride from Tintagel Island to Glastonbury. He and Fiona had arrived at the Thistle Down Inn a short time ago. She left him in the inn's barn with instructions to bathe before they continued their journey to find his future bride. In addition, she asked him to shave his beard and trim his hair. He agreed to bathe, but declined to shave his beard and cut his hair. It had taken him a year to grow both out.

Fiona had been vague about the location where he would meet a potential bride, saying it was a land far away. A year ago, Nessa had described the place he had met Madeline in the same way. Fiona had not, however, been vague about why he needed to bathe. According to the matchmaker, he smelled worse than his horse.

Nessa had made the same bath requirement last year before he met Madeline. Perhaps it was some sort of matchmaker rule.

Madeline.

Why did she haunt his waking and sleeping hours? He could not stop thinking about her—her smile, those expressive eyes, and the way she cared for her grandmother.

People say that a memory fades over time. For him, his short time with Madeline had grown more vivid— and more painful—with the passage of time.

He stripped off his jacket and shirt and shrugged out of the sleeves of his undergarment, tossing them over the gate of the horse's stall. A bath in the dead of winter was madness. Bathing was a springtime event. He scooped cold water from the horse's trough and splashed it over his face and chest. Tensing, he sucked in his breath and let out a string of colorful oaths. The water was as cold as the walls of Tintagel Castle.

His horse nickered in the stall nearby, and two of the other horses joined in the chorus. Colin pulled back the wet hair from his face. "Careful, Dragon, or you will be next." He dived his hands into the water and hesitated. "What are you doing?"

Colin rested his hands on the sides of the trough. He needed to find Excalibur. Then, and only then, could he think about finding a bride. Madeline's image shimmered in his thoughts again. He did not want just anyone. He wanted Madeline.

A woman screamed and burst into the barn. Flame-red hair cascaded over her shoulders like waves crashing over the shores beneath his castle. He stood rooted to the ground. What magic was this? He knew it was Madeline. He had been thinking about her and she appeared as though conjured from his thoughts. He must be dreaming. That was the only explanation.

Still...

He walked toward her slowly.

Madeline slammed the door closed, bolted it, and spun around, only to plow into Colin.

He caught her around the waist before she fell, his arms holding her against him. His breath caught in his throat. Vulnerability and strength shone in her eyes.

Those qualities added to those he already knew.

"Madeline…"

She pushed against him and stepped back. "How do you know my name?" She took in his appearance, her voice rising higher. "You're naked. And wet." She stumbled away from him until her back was against the wall near the door. She grabbed the pitchfork leaning there and pointed it toward him, jabbing at the air. "Stay away from me."

He held up his hands in peace. "I will not harm you."

"Uh-huh. Sociopaths say the same thing before they attack." She used the pitchfork to point in the direction of his clothes. "Put on your clothes."

Men beat on the door, demanding to enter. "Open the door."

She jumped and whirled to face the noise, her expression like that of a cornered animal.

Chapter Nineteen

She was surrounded.

The three men pounded on the wooden door, shouting to let them inside. Horses neighed in protest, and behind her the half-naked man had extinguished the lantern, turning the barn as black as a judge's robe. Metal scraped against metal as he pulled his sword from its sheath.

There had been something vaguely familiar about him around the eyes, the athletic way he moved, and in the tone of his voice. But it was difficult to know what he looked like under all that hair. On the other hand, there was no mystery regarding his body. The hard feel of it against hers would be forever burned in her memory.

Focus.

She gripped the handle of her pitchfork tighter, until her fingers ached. The moon that moments ago had filtered its light through the cracks had now ducked behind clouds as though afraid to witness what might happen below.

The banging on the door ceased.

Muffled voices drifted away on the wind. Had they left? The bearded man was so close she heard his breathing. It was slow and even, as though he hadn't a worry in the world.

Her pulse raced until she was gasping for breath.

One danger averted. Another in its place.

She was alone in a barn with a man who looked like he could take on a dozen men and survive. What chance would she have to fight him off if he attacked her?

Horses nickered in the stalls nearby. The bearded man whispered soothing words to the animals to quiet them. The calmness in his voice worked on her as well. She hoped his way with animals was a sign that he was one of the good guys.

The wind whispered through the rafters, sending a chill over her skin. She bit down on her lip to keep the panic at bay, remembering that one of her father's clients owned a horse ranch but the guy was a real creep.

"Focus," she repeated under her breath.

At her mother's insistence, she'd taken a self-defense course in case she was attacked in the parking garage after office hours. The instructor advised gripping her keys through her fingers and using them as a weapon to drag against her assailant's face. He called the technique *The Wolverine*, after the comic book character who could will long knives to emerge from his hands. The goal was to use the keys as weapons and then run like hell.

Except she didn't have keys. She had something better, a pitchfork. She wouldn't have to stand close to attack.

A loud boom split the air. The door shuddered from the impact of the blow. The men had returned and were trying to break down the door. She gripped the handle of her weapon and willed her trembling hands to steady. She refused to behave like a victim. She would fight.

The battering ram thundered against the door, breaking through wood slats. The three men cheered and shouted that one more thrust and they would be through. They stopped to make a lewd remark, suggesting they intended to do the same to Madeline.

"Cave dwellers," she said.

The bearded man snickered behind her, startling her. Was he agreeing with the men outside or her?

The battering ram smashed through. The men tore away the wood to clear an entrance as Madeline stood her ground. There was no place to hide.

The man from the tavern stood on the threshold, holding a lantern in his left hand and a knife in his right. The bearded man had come up alongside her, and his presence shook their confidence.

"Be on your way, Henry," the bearded man said in a tone that set the hair on the nape of Madeline's neck on end. He turned toward Madeline. "What did you call them?" His expression hardened. "I remember. And take those cave dwellers with you. The Lady Madeline is not for you."

"Saving a damsel in distress, I see. I'm not surprised. You are forever the chivalrous knight. You do not belong in this century, cousin. You should have been born in King Arthur's time. Had you been, I've no doubt 'twould have been you to pull Excalibur from the stone, and not Arthur. Ironic that it is the same sword you need to break Merlin's Curse."

The bearded man raised his sword. "I do not wish to fight you."

"You were always too serious. She will not want you once she learns of Merlin's Curse. No woman would. Nor will you find Excalibur. Save us all a lot of trouble and tell your father to declare me his heir."

"Madeline stays with me, and as for the rest, your brother the priest should have told you that it is a sin to covet what belongs to another man."

"You have sealed your fate. If you want the woman, you will have to fight for her."

"You know me, cousin. I never run from a fight."

"So be it." Henry set the lantern aside and shot a glance toward his men. "Take him."

The bearded man had sheathed his sword and now leapt between Madeline and Henry's men, tackling them to the ground.

Henry lunged toward her as she gripped the handle of the pitchfork and rushed to meet him. She aimed for his chest.

He swerved away, but not in time. The pitchfork tines grazed his side. He yelped in pain, holding his side as blood seeped between his fingers. He roared, holding his knife out in front of him, and charged.

The bearded man jumped from behind her and pinned Henry against the wall. "Who sent you? You would not have dared this on your own."

Madeline slipped into the shadows as the conversation between the two men continued. She needed to escape this madness. In retrospect, the idea of traveling back in time to try to find Colin Penrose had been one of her dumber ideas. Right up there along with thinking it was a good idea to debate her English history professor, who was from Britain, that Queen Elizabeth's moniker of Virgin Queen was symbolic, not literal.

The men's voices rose in anger as Madeline edged

to the back of the barn, feeling her way along the wall. There had to be another way out.

"This is not over," Henry shouted.

"That is the first thing we agree upon, cousin," the bearded man shot back as the men left, taking their lantern.

Once more the barn was pitch black. The bearded man swore, and then something struck a wall as though he had hit it with his fist. He swore again.

She lifted her pitchfork out in front of her and pressed against the wall.

Light flickered to life from a lantern.

The bearded man held it at chest level, gazing straight at her. "My cousin and his men have left. I fear they will return, so it is best we leave." He paused. "I am Colin Edward Penrose the Sixth."

Chapter Twenty

Madeline opened her eyes. She lay on the damp, straw-packed ground. She had fainted—a first. The bearded man—Colin Edward Penrose the Sixth, she corrected—stared down at her as though she were indeed, a damsel who fainted at the slightest provocation.

She'd found him, was her first thought, and a close second was, Now what? Her pulse rate jumped a notch. She was in his world, and her first impression was that it was more dangerous than she had ever imagined. Nessa had cautioned her not to let anyone know that she had time traveled to the fifteenth century. Did Nessa also mean Colin?

He had traveled to Madeline's time, she reasoned, but other than Colin behaving old-world formal, he hadn't appeared disoriented. Perhaps that was because her mother's guests were dressed as he had been, and the Matchmaker Café had been transformed into a medieval-style ballroom. She decided to play it safe until she talked to Fiona.

She pushed to her elbows, and Colin helped her sit.

"Are you able to stand?" he said, worry lines deepening across his forehead.

"I think so. I never faint," she said, more to herself than Colin. "I didn't recognize you with the beard." She was nervous. She knew next to nothing about the man.

"I prefer a beard in winter," he said as though that was all the explanation he needed to give. He helped her to her feet, keeping his arm around her waist. "Did you hear something?"

She moved away from him enough to break their connection. She couldn't hear anything over her panic-driven heartbeat. She needed to talk to Fiona, and according to maps, Tintagel was nearly two hundred kilometers from Glastonbury.

"I must reach Tintagel Castle," she blurted. "I'm to meet someone there."

Colin turned back to her, his eyes narrowing as he scratched his chin. Madeline imagined she saw fleas moving around in the bushy beard. She grimaced as he said, "I too am bound for the island castle, but there is business I must conduct in Glastonbury first. I can order you a carriage, although I advise against traveling alone. If you care to wait until I finish, I will take you myself."

Should she go alone, take her chances, or go with Colin? She prided herself on navigating big cities like New York, San Francisco, and Seattle. But this was the fifteenth century, and she couldn't call 9-1-1 if things turned sideways. Reading about the century's culture and living in it were two different things. The fish-out-of-water cliché was an understatement.

The dark expression in Henry's eyes flashed in her thoughts. "I can wait," she said, her voice not as steady as she would have liked.

"Do you smell something burning?"

Across the barn, flames spread out from under the gap between the walls and the dirt floor. Fire jumped to a tinder-dry stack of hay. The horses whinnied and pawed the packed earth. Colin raced to swing the barn doors open.

"I suspect Henry set a fire from outside," Colin yelled. "Get out of here before the roof collapses." Colin snatched a horse blanket from the stall and plunged it into the water trough. He beat the blanket against the flames as another fire started a short distance away from the first. Waves of heat and smoke clogged the air.

Three more fires sprang out along the edge of the barn like falling dominos. Madeline ignored Colin's order to save herself, grabbed another horse blanket, and repeated Colin's actions, taking on a fire next to the one he tried to beat out.

This wasn't a coincidence. She suspected Henry was attempting to burn down the barn with her and Colin inside. But why? Had they mistaken her for someone else? There was also bad blood between Colin and his cousin. But enough for Henry to want Colin dead?

"Leave!" Colin shouted again. His voice was layered with concern.

"I can help you with the horses," she shouted over the roar of the flames.

Fire ignited on the roof, burning through the thatch and timbers in no time. It raced up the center and side posts and spread down the walls. At any moment it would eat through the support beams.

The horses reared, pawing against their locked stalls.

Flames lit up the barn, turning night into day as their hunger consumed the walls of the barn. Timbers cracked, then crashed onto the ground. Colin fought to unlock the stalls, the horses inside becoming more and more frantic. Their eyes wide with fear and nostrils flaring, they reared on their haunches and pawed the air and the gates of their stalls.

Madeline reached Colin's side. Each time he tried to get close to their stalls, they reared, too panicked to understand that he was there to help them escape. She instinctively knew he would not leave them. But if he didn't free the animals soon, they would all perish.

"I can help," Madeline repeated over the thunder of the flames. "I'm good with animals."

She hoped having a continuing assortment of dogs, cats, one hamster, and a goldfish as she grew up supported her "good with animals" assertion.

She reached out to the nearest horse, a black stallion with a white face. She spoke to the animal in the same tone she had used when her new puppy had been frightened by Fourth of July fireworks. Instead of joining the neighborhood celebrations with her friends, she had stayed with Charlie all night. Once the stallion with the white face was calmed, she rushed to the other two horses, a mare with kind, brown eyes and one with a golden mane. The tone of her words quieted the animals enough to give Colin the opportunity he needed.

"Stand back from the stalls," he yelled to Madeline. He unsheathed his sword, lifted the blade over his head and brought it down in an arc onto the locks on the first stall. The force of his blow broke the first set of locks. He hurried to the others, while roof timbers crashed to the ground, sending soot and smoke into the air.

With the locks all released, he swung the stall

doors open, pulling Madeline out of the way as two of the horses raced past them and out of the barn to safety, kicking up straw in their wake. The mare with the kind, brown eyes stayed behind, too frightened to move.

Flames leapt in Madeline's direction as a section of the roof collapsed a short distance away. She screamed and brought her arms up to cover her head.

Chapter Twenty-One

Colin rushed to Madeline's side and covered her with a wet blanket. "Can you run?"

She gave him a quick nod as he grabbed the mare's reins and led her out of the barn at a jog.

Waves of heat and choking smoke closed in around Colin. Keeping Madeline and the mare close, he raced in the same direction the two horses had fled moments before. The barn creaked and groaned. He kept running, thankful Madeline kept pace.

Once clear of the barn, the mare broke free of Colin's grip and bolted toward the village.

The roof collapsed, sending sparks flying into the air. Several landed a short distance away but sizzled and died out on the rain-soaked ground. Another landed on Colin's arm and caught his sleeve on fire.

"Hold still," Madeline shouted and used the blanket to smother the flames.

Shouts from the townspeople lifted behind him as they streamed out of adjoining buildings and houses, trying to contain the flames before they spread. Orders to form water brigades were replaced with screams as sections of the walls crashed to the ground.

"We have to keep moving," he said.

Once clear of the barn and the intense heat of the flames, cold air rose up like a wall. The horses were long gone. He figured his horse would not stop until he reached the cliffs overlooking Tintagel Island.

With Madeline beside him, Colin pushed through and kept running. If the fire gained a foothold, it would spread.

Madeline had a quiet beauty and strength about her that promised to grow with each moment he spent with her. He had felt its allure the moment he first saw her. Her uniqueness had intensified when she threatened Henry with a pitchfork and then stayed to help him save the horses. But the reason why Henry had been so determined to have Madeline was a mystery.

Henry had never been the sort to pursue a woman who was not interested in him. And why had he gone to such lengths to try to kill Colin? Merlin's Curse followed the Penrose heir. Why would anyone want that kind of burden?

Slowing his pace, he headed toward the river. Somewhere in the crowd his cousin would be holding a vigil to determine whether or not Colin and Madeline had escaped. When the flames died, leaving only ash and ruin, his cousin would search for bodies. That his cousin would go to this extreme to try to kill him had taken Colin by surprise. His cousin had joked in the past that upon Colin's death, he would be happy to risk the death of any woman he married if it meant possessing the Penrose lands and immense wealth. The boast always came after a night of drinking, and Colin had never taken it seriously. What if his cousin had tired of waiting?

What was certain was that after tonight his cousin would not stop. He would assume Colin would know he started the fire. Colin estimated that he and Madeline had until dawn before his cousin started hunting for them.

The moon shimmered over the banks of the river as rain began to fall again.

He slowed, and Madeline followed his lead.

She walked over to the river and dipped her hands into the water to wash the soot from her hands and face. "We should look for the horses."

"They are halfway to Tintagel by now. Were you burned?"

"I don't think so. You might have been, though. I'm worried about your hands, and take off your jacket. It's good you grabbed it, but I want to look at your arm."

He did as she had asked and let her push his hands into the freezing river. A few times he tried to pull his hands out of the water, but each time she shook her head and said, "Not yet," while she examined his shoulders and arms for burns. No one had ever fussed over him before, and it felt good.

His first impression of her at the Christmas Eve ball had been that she was a kind woman in need of protection. Then when he saw her again in the barn, it was as though another version of her had appeared. Henry and his men attacked, but she joined in the fight rather than standing on the sidelines. She barely reached his shoulders, but she was as brave as men twice her size. Her features were delicate and her skin pale, as though she rarely saw the sun, yet she ran alongside him as though she had spent her life running along paths and cliffs. The expression in her forest-green eyes was kind and courageous. She was a woman of contrasts.

She had stood up to his cousin and speared him

with her pitchfork, risked her life to help the horses, and had run alongside him as though her strength were limitless. Even now, after all she'd endured, it was not fear reflected in her eyes but blossoming defiance.

"Stop staring at me," she said. "You're making me nervous. You can take your hands out of the water. You should be okay, and I didn't find any burns on your body. If you start to blister, let me know."

The moon caught the flames of her hair and the curve of her neck as she reached for his jacket and held it up for him. She was breathtaking.

He stayed her hand. "You have examined my body for burns. Perhaps I should examine yours as well?"

Her lips curled in a smirk. "Ha-ha. I'm just fine, funny man. Nice try. Put your jacket on." She grew serious. "Henry burning down the barn with us inside wasn't just about my rejecting him."

"You are correct." Colin shrugged on his jacket. "Henry's actions tonight baffled me. His family owns more lands than mine, and yet he covets Tintagel Castle. In addition, I have never known Henry to behave the way he did toward any woman who rejected him."

"It's clear he wants you dead."

Colin held her gaze and pulled her to her feet, nodding. "I have put you in danger. Will you ever forgive me?"

Chapter Twenty-Two

Madeline forced one foot in front of the other along the tree-shrouded path and concentrated on staying awake. It seemed as though she and Colin had left the river days ago instead of hours. By the position of the moon, it looked like it was close to two or three in the morning.

Colin had asked if she could forgive him for putting her in danger. There was nothing to forgive. She'd entered this world of her own free will. Well, that was not entirely true. Nessa had pushed her. Still, she'd agreed to go. Up until she'd crossed the threshold from her century to this one, she'd had a romanticized vision of this time period. She should have known better.

He hacked his way through the dark forest as though it were a jungle and he a big game hunter. According to Colin, they needed to stay off the main road.

Madeline locked her arm around Colin's, fearful she might lose sight of him if he walked too far in front of her. A short time ago it had begun to rain again and she was soaked to the skin. She'd clamped her teeth down to keep them from chattering away like a model in five-inch heels strutting over a tile floor. It was important to her that she pulled her own weight and was not a burden to him. She couldn't imagine how Colin must feel, knowing that someone he had known all his life wanted him dead.

An icy breeze, with the promise of snow, slipped through the trees. She shivered and tightened her hold on Colin's arm.

"You are cold." He put his free hand over hers.

The warmth of his touch was reassuring, and she leaned in closer. Her teeth chattered as she said, "I'm okay."

His arm was around her, holding her close, and then in an instant he picked her up and cradled her in his arms. "We are almost to the inn. It is not as grand as the one in Glastonbury, but I have known the owner since I was a child, and she will be happy to offer us a warm meal and a place to rest."

"Please put me down," she said. "I'm too heavy."

He chuckled, and the sound rumbled through her as she snuggled against his chest. He chuckled again. "You are not heavy, milady. You are like air in my arms."

"And you are a big fat liar."

"You doubt my word? I am a knight. We cannot lie. Besides, only a fool would forfeit the chance to hold a beautiful woman in his arms. I am many things, but I am no fool."

"You are gallant, like my own personal Sir Galahad. Thank you," she said, yawning. The will to fight and insist she could walk on her own dissolved as his warmth enveloped her. Although his clothes were soaked through like hers, the heat of his body spread across her in delicious waves. "You're so warm."

"There are many who would disagree. I'm considered cold and distant. Sleep, dear Madeline. We will be there soon. The inn is over the next rise."

Her thoughts lingered on what he'd said about people thinking him cold and distant. Timothy had given almost that same excuse as the reason he'd cheated on her. She and this man from the past had something in common. They were surrounded by idiots. She yawned and sighed as her eyelids grew heavy.

****

"Lady Madeline, please awaken. We have arrived at the inn."

A man's voice, rich and low, seemed to come from a long way away. A nice voice. A confident voice. A voice she could trust. The judgment attached to the voice infiltrated her thoughts as she wondered why she'd connected all those emotions to a voice. She had heard that voice before.

She stretched and tried to drift back to sleep. She leaned against something solid. Had she fallen asleep at the desk in her office? She didn't want to wake up. She'd been dreaming, and although there'd been adventure and danger, it had taken a romantic turn. She had been transported back in time, been attacked by thugs, and almost been burned alive. The man who had rescued her had long hair, an unkempt beard and smelled like wet horse. She doubted her father would approve, because of the man's casual association with bathing and shaving. Had that been the reason for her attraction?

She couldn't be in her office. She smelled of burning wood and beer, and she heard the clatter of dishes and the hum of conversation. Her office was dead quiet and smelled like disinfectant.

Someone shook her shoulder. "Wake up," the man with the deep voice repeated.

Her eyes closed, still holding onto the remnants of the dream, she yawned. She was sitting. Worst fear confirmed. She'd dozed off at work. How embarrassing.

Madeline yawned again, stretched, and opened her eyes.

A man knelt before her, his hands on her shoulders, resembling a wild man from the mountains. She recognized him at once. Colin. She hadn't been dreaming.

The events of the last few hours rushed back. Nessa had pushed her over a mist-shrouded threshold into the fifteenth century, she'd been attacked, then trapped in a burning building. She'd been saved, but things could always get worse. She had to get back.

She scooted against the back of the wooden chair and gripped its sides. She was in what looked like an inn in the Middle Ages—low ceiling, candles on the tables, a few wall sconces, and a fireplace to her right. Beef-and-herb broth bubbled in an iron pot over the fire, and a loaf of fresh baked bread was on the table next to where Madeline had been sleeping. Her mother would love this place.

"Is something wrong with your wife?" a middle-aged woman asked, holding a tray with steaming soup and more bread. The woman's face was as round and dark as the bread, and she wore a clean apron over an ankle-length, earth-toned dress.

Colin took the tray from the woman. "It has been a long day, Sarah. The Lady Madeline and I will go to our room now. Thank you for the meal. You are most generous."

"'Tis I who am grateful, sire. You have always

been kind to me and mine." Her voice lowered, and the worry lines around her eyes deepened. "Your wife be but a little thing of skin and bone. 'Tis a mighty curse your family bears. Be she strong enough if a babe is born?"

Colin's voice turned to steel. "Sarah..."

Sarah wiped her hands on her apron, nodding. "Aye, I overstepped my place and beg your forgiveness. I'll leave the two of you in peace." She patted Madeline on the cheek. "Ye have a fine man here with Colin, none finer, and I count my blessed Willy in the mix, God rest his soul."

Two men who wore hooded cloaks entered the inn, and Sarah rushed to greet them. The more clean-shaven of the two talked to Sarah while the other scanned the room.

"We should go." Colin nodded for Madeline to follow him toward the stairs that led to the second floor.

She hurried to catch up. "Did Sarah just call me your wife?"

Chapter Twenty-Three

The stairs creaked with each step Madeline took. She lifted her skirts and followed Colin. A long dress was fun to wear when standing still but a challenge in which to run or climb stairs. She missed her jeans, yoga pants, and jogging clothes.

It hadn't escaped her notice that Colin ignored her question whether Sarah had called her his wife, or how concerned he had looked when the two men had arrived. She hadn't recognized the men, but that didn't mean Henry hadn't hired them to hunt for her and Colin.

Colin reached the landing of the third floor of the inn and shouldered the door open. He looked like a man consumed in thought. Whatever he was thinking, it didn't look good. The room, on the other hand, was a surprise. Although smaller than her walk-in closet, and stone-cold, it was as neat and clean as Sarah's apron.

There was a twin-size bed against the wall, with a threadbare blanket that might once have been red. The only other furnishings were a round table and two chairs. Outside the window, the rosy-pink shades of dawn broke through the mist and offered relief from the gray.

"Red sky at night, sailors' delight. Red sky in the morning, sailors take warning," Madeline said, reciting the old saying. She shivered and tucked her hands into the folds of her dress.

"Did you say something?" Colin deposited the tray of food on the table, broke off a chunk of bread, and crossed to close the shutters on the window.

"It was nothing." For the moment she decided to let Sarah's comment pass, and asking about the two men would only make her more afraid. Colin looked worried enough for both of them. "Can I help? I can build a fire."

Colin's mouth turned up at the corners. "I have no doubt you can do whatever you set your mind to. Try to rest. We may have to leave in a hurry."

She pulled out the chair closest to the fireplace and sat down. "We're not safe yet, are we?"

Colin bent over the hearth as he added wood from the stack nearby. "You are observant. The men downstairs might not be looking for us." The words not said hung in the air.

Madeline blew on her hands to warm them. "But they could be."

He nodded and lit the fire.

Smoke curled over the kindling and spilled out into the room.

Madeline coughed, and the smoke burned her eyes as she rushed over and opened the shutters. She waved her arms to try to direct the smoke outside. "Is it supposed to do that?"

He threw a blanket over the wood and smothered the fire. A muscle flexed along his jaw line. "There must be a nest in the chimney."

He ducked his head into the hearth. He edged in closer, half hidden from view. Muffled swear words joined twigs, clumps of dirt, and feathers as he pulled a bird's nest out of the chimney. He emerged, his face covered in soot. "That should help."

Within a matter of seconds, Colin had restarted the fire, with only a few wisps of smoke as a reminder of the bird's nest. She held her hands over the building flames, casting a glance toward Colin as he knelt to add more wood. He had long eyelashes and a strong, Roman-style nose that she hadn't noticed before. Her pulse quickened. He was a handsome man, even with the beard.

"Well done," she said, motioning to the hearth and receiving a grin in return

"Next time I will accept your offer to help me build a fire."

Her face warmed under his gaze as she focused on the flames. "Why did you tell Sarah we were married?"

He dusted his hands off on his pants. "Sarah turned away a couple because they were not married. You and I are bone-tired and need rest, and I did not relish the idea of sleeping outside in a rainstorm. We still have a long way to go before we reach Tintagel. Telling Sarah that we were married seemed logical. And when I told Sarah we were married, she also offered the loan of her horses when her son returns."

Madeline glanced over at the bed hugging the far wall. Up to now, Colin had been a perfect gentleman. Was that about to change?

Colin rose from the hearth and crossed over to the table, took one of the bowls of steaming soup from the tray, and sat down.

Madeline sat also and reached for a bowl of soup as well. The layered barley, potato, and rosemary blended together in a welcoming aroma. "The soup smells amazing."

He scooped up another spoonful of soup. "We can't stay long. This is the only inn for miles, and my cousin will be searching for us when he confirms that we did not die in the fire, if he has not done so already."

She took a spoonful and sighed with pleasure. "This is good."

He grinned. "I told you."

As she continued eating, she said, "Why does your cousin want us dead?" She knew she'd asked him this question before.

He finished his slice of bread and reached for more, shrugging. "He wants something that belongs to me."

Madeline dunked the bread in the thick soup and concentrated on her food. Was Colin talking about a woman? Was he married? Panic shot through her faster than lightning. "Are you married?"

His grin returned. "No. Are you?"

With a mouthful of bread, she shook her head, licking the crumbs from her mouth.

His eyebrows drew together. "How is that possible? You are an intelligent, beautiful woman, filled with spirit and courage. I would think your father would have had many suitors eager to marry you. Are you poor then, despite the fine quality of your clothes?"

She laughed aloud. Her father would have bristled at Colin's question. Her father prided himself on the things his money could buy, from memberships at the Seattle Yacht Club and the Glendale Golf Course to owning a waterfront compound on Lake Washington that made the tech billionaires envious.

Colin cocked his head. "Did I say something

humorous?"

She tamed her laughter into a chuckle. "My father considers himself very wealthy and has a man chosen for me that most women would jump at the chance to marry."

"Except you."

She set her spoon aside. "Except me. My father says that love doesn't last, but he does believe in mergers. For him, marriage is a business proposition between prominent families for their mutual benefit."

Colin rubbed his eyes with the back of his hand. "Then we are more alike than you think. My father has made similar remarks over the years, although he married for love. The woman of his heart died giving me life. My father never recovered from the loss, and I believe he does not want me to experience the same pain." Colin yawned and stood, the chair scraping against the wood floor as he walked over to the bed and reached for the blanket. "As much as I would like to continue our conversation, it is time for us to go to bed."

"I'm not sleeping with you."

He paused, his eyebrows knitting together in a frown. Then he nodded. "It is not my intent that we share a bed in that regard, though I admit that I have never wanted a woman more than I want you. You and I will not sleep together. I will take the floor."

His words tolled in her ears like giant bells that wouldn't stop ringing. He'd said he wanted her. She gulped for breath. She took the blanket from him and shook her head. "I'm not tired, and you look dead on your feet. I had a nice nap in your arms, remember?"

His smile lit up his face, tugging at her heart. "A

memory I'll cherish. I was sorry to see the inn."

Her face heated at his warm glance. When she closed her eyes, she knew she'd be able to imagine how his arms had felt around her—warm and protective.

He yawned and sank down on the bed, and within seconds he was asleep.

Her heart hammered in her chest as though it might burst as she covered Colin with the blanket and stepped back. His features relaxed in sleep, making him appear younger, as though the weight of the world had slipped away. As though he wasn't being hunted by someone who wanted him killed.

Colin had said he wanted her. In the same breath he'd said he wouldn't sleep with her. Then he'd flirted with her. Her emotions ping-ponged in a thousand different directions at the same time.

Madeline drew up a chair beside the bed, feeling as though she wanted to keep vigil over him. He was hiding something. She could sense it in the same way she knew when her clients lied to her during the first interview. "What secrets are you hiding, my handsome beast?" she said as she reached over and pulled the blanket over his shoulder.

Chapter Twenty-Four

A soft knock on the door startled Madeline awake.

She pitched forward in her chair and slammed into the table. Fully awake, she glanced toward Colin. He'd heard the sound as well and had headed toward the door.

Colin listened at the door, and then said, "It is Sarah." He left to see what she had to say, leaving Madeline alone.

At first she'd been afraid to sleep and had eaten only a few bits of Sarah's bread. Then she had spent the last few hours alternating between pacing and keeping the fire from dying out. She'd sat down to rest, and the last thing she remembered was hearing Colin snore.

Her stomach rumbled. The soup was cold and congealed, and the fire was a pile of ash. She tore off a chunk of bread, wondering if Sarah had any cheese.

Colin reentered the room and grabbed his jacket from the bed. "They found us."

Madeline kept her voice low. "How do you know?"

He crossed toward the window in the room and peered out through the breaks between the shutters. "I asked Sarah to let me know if anyone came looking for us. She came to warn us." He cracked the shutters open and glanced down at the ground and then in the direction of a cluster of oak trees hugging the roofline. "I do not see them. They must have stabled their horses out back. How good are you at climbing trees?"

She'd done a lot of new things in the last twenty-four hours. Climbing trees would be one more. She'd like to brag to Colin that as a child she'd climbed trees on a regular basis and as an adult had spent her vacations rock climbing. None of that was true. She preferred reading about people doing the impossible and participating in heart-stopping, nail-biting adventures, while she sat in the comfort of her apartment with a cup of hot cocoa and a chocolate brownie.

She twisted the folds of her dress in her hands. "I'm not dressed for climbing trees," she ventured. "Maybe they'll go away without searching the rooms."

He drew back from the window; his gaze traveled the length of her and settled on her eyes. "They will search the rooms. Of that, I am certain. My cousin is very thorough. When we were younger, we would play hide-and-seek with children our own age, and the only person better at the game than me was Henry. Fear not, I will not let you fall."

She managed a short, clipped laugh. In movies and romance novels, that is what heroes always said. In stories based on real life, however, it didn't always go as well. She knew he wouldn't want to drop her. He looked confident and sure of himself. She doubted he had ever failed at anything. He probably was the smartest kid, the fastest runner, and the one who never had to worry about a date for the prom.

Madeline nodded and pressed her lips together to keep them from trembling. She nodded again. "I'm holding you to your promise."

****

Downstairs, voices raised in anger confronted an angry Sarah as Colin explored his options. He knew Sarah would delay the search of her inn as long as possible. Madeline had moved to a corner of the room and was in the process of removing her long belt and rolling up the sleeves of her gown. It was clear that the gown was not suited for climbing. Even if she wore men's breeches, the slope of the roof—and the ice on it—made the task challenging. He had promised he would not let her fall, and he vowed to keep that pledge.

Colin had known Sarah most of his life. The first time they met he was six years old. He had run away from the castle when a tutor insisted that he learn Latin because it was the language of the Church and the civilized world. Colin almost acquiesced until the monk added that it would be useful if Colin became a priest, thus avoiding Merlin's Curse. After a day and a half of wandering through the forest, he was hungry and tired when he'd discovered Sarah's inn. She had taken him in, but recognizing the young heir, she had sent word to his father.

Colin had learned two things that day: most people were kindhearted, and if he were to run away again, he would need more supplies.

Sarah's voice vaulted higher. Madeline flinched at the sound. He noted that although she hid her shaking hands in the folds of her gown, her eyes were steady. The woman had courage.

Madeline used his knife to cut away a generous portion of cloth from the hem of her gown. She did it as though she cared not for the ruin of such an expensive garment. Was it because she had so many that the loss of one meant so little? The women he had known, and granted there were not many, were as protective regarding their garments as he was about his weapons.

She stood in a shadowed corner and removed layers of white underskirts. She had mentioned that she had had difficulty running in so many clothes. The comment had seemed odd. The ladies he knew seldom ran. They glided across rooms in slow, calculated steps that reminded him of swans paddling over a summer pond.

He caught a glimpse of a shapely leg, as well as her smile when she discovered him staring. He gave her a curt nod of approval as though that was the reason he had glanced her way. Her raised eyebrow and the tilt of her smile suggested she knew otherwise.

Reluctantly, he turned away and concentrated on their escape route. This woman was an enigma, a puzzle with missing pieces. She was beautiful, and though many women possessed this gift, her beauty was not only on the surface. She glowed from within, and it reflected in her eyes and in the melodic tone of her voice.

He had promised to protect her and not let her fall. It had not been an idle promise. He strained to see into the shadows of the forest for signs of danger, his need to protect her growing by the hour.

Madeline returned his knife. "How long do you think Sarah will be able to prevent the men downstairs from searching the inn?"

"Not long. You should keep the blade." He held back that she might need it if something happened to him.

Madeline looped her belt through the knife's sheath

and then reattached her belt around her waist. "Our staying places Sarah and everyone here in danger."

He was taken back at her concern for others when her life was in jeopardy. "You are correct. The voices have quieted, and I suspect it is because they are planning how best to search the inn. If you are ready, we must leave before they begin."

"Do you think they've hurt Sarah?"

His jaw clenched as he strained to listen. The conversation below had been reduced to the clattering of dishes, random laughter, and the scraping of chairs. The usual noise for a busy establishment. "Even my cousin is not foolish enough to risk his own death by harming Sarah. Still…"

"Well, then we should leave right away. I'm ready."

He took in Madeline's transformed appearance in awe. Her fierce expression reminded him of the legendary Amazons. In addition to shortening her gown and rolling up her sleeves, she had arranged her hair into a single braid and stood with her fists perched on her hips as though ready for battle.

She cocked her head. "Why are you staring at me? You keep doing that."

He blinked. Why indeed? If he told her she was the image of a warrior queen, would she be offended? He had no way of knowing. Women wanted to be obedient and compliant, or so his father and the Church preached. He had a strong feeling that Madeline's true nature chafed against both of those things.

But Colin also recognized the hesitation in Madeline's eyes. He had seen it in the men he led into battle. They trusted him with their survival; they trusted that he would make the right decision. His father had told him that leaders must know the strength as well as the weakness of their men. Madeline was stronger than she realized.

Madeline would follow him out the window, of that he was certain. Once pushed against a wall, rather than bowing to defeat she was as brave and determined as his best soldiers. But as with his soldiers, Colin would choose the path that offered the safest outcome.

The edges of sunlight spread its fingers over the high grass. Men's voices corrupted the waking dawn as they slashed at the underbrush with their swords, searching for Colin and Madeline. The men's attack on the woods chased birds into the air and rabbits and squirrels deeper into the safety of the forest. Escaping by way of the window while the men patrolled the perimeter of the inn was no longer a viable option. If Colin and Madeline survived the jump to the ground, they would be in full sight of his cousin's men. Colin needed a diversion.

"New plan," he said. "We are going to start a fire."

"Wait a second." Her forehead wrinkled in frown lines. "What is it with this place and fires?" she said under her breath. "Is jumping from a three-story building not dangerous enough, but you have to add fire to the mix? What about all the people in the inn, or that you will be burning down Sarah's business? There has to be another way."

Her concern for the welfare of others no longer came as a surprise. "I will warn Sarah and pay for the repair of her inn. No one will be harmed, I promise."

He swept his arm to include the window. "My cousin's men are outside, and instead of one of

England's notoriously gray days, there is bright sunshine. The moment we leave, we will be captured. We need a diversion."

She reached for one of the undergarments she had discarded and looped it over her arm, heading toward the hearth. "We don't need to burn down the inn. All we need is smoke." Setting her undergarments aside, she scooped up the bird's nest and twigs Colin had discarded. "We fill the room with smoke. There is still danger it will spark into a full-fledged fire, but it will at least give people time, and the smoke will cover our escape."

Colin knelt beside Madeline and helped her stuff the chimney. "You would make a good general."

"Did you ever have any doubts?"

Chapter Twenty-Five

The room filled with choking smoke as Madeline stood next to the windowsill. Colin was already outside, as calm and happy as a mountain goat on Mount Everest. She wanted to kick him.

"Stay close to me," Colin said. "Our goal is to climb along the eaves until we reach the side that faces the forest. The roofline slopes lower there, and the drop to the ground is not as far." He crawled farther out onto the roof, drawing her alongside him.

A gray veil covered the sun as it rose higher above the horizon. Madeline climbed out onto the slate roof, trying not to look down but failing in the attempt. Behind her, smoke filled the room they had occupied. Their plan was working.

Mirroring Colin, she inched out from the window and, with her back against the building, crept along the ledge that ran the length of the inn. Freezing wind, laced with shards of ice, lashed against Madeline's skin. She clamped her lips and regretted that she hadn't used some of her gown's cloth to wrap around her hands. Colin moved as fluidly as a cat along the ledge, with no discernable sign of fear. She, on the other hand, was drenched in sweat.

Colin eased down, squatting on the ledge, and whispered, "We are at the roof's lowest point. When we land, do not stop. Run into the forest as fast as you can."

Madeline looked at the ground. It didn't look any closer to her than when they'd started. "Are you insane?" she whispered back. "We'll break our necks."

"I will catch you."

She rolled her eyes. "Of course you will," she said in a deadly even tone. "What happens if you break your neck first? How will you catch me then? Or what if your crazy cousin is waiting for us? Have you thought of that?"

He seemed to consider her words. "You offer good points. Be sure you land on me when you jump. That way if the fall kills me, my body will break your fall."

She hated how practical he sounded, but worse was his message. It sounded as though he thought his life were expendable. His voice wasn't laced with sadness. It didn't shake or hint that he wanted credit for his sacrifice. For some reason, that made her mad.

She pinched him on the arm. "You have to promise me one more thing."

"We do not have time…"

"I'm not moving until you promise." With his nod, she said, "Promise you won't die."

Chapter Twenty-Six

Smoke curled out of the windows of several third-floor rooms as Madeline ran after Colin into the forest. The plan had worked better than they'd hoped. Smoke had spread quickly, billowing out the windows and engulfing the stairs. People ran from the inn. The panic as well as the smoke aided in Colin and Madeline's escape.

Madeline looked over her shoulder for any hint of flames as they increased their distance from the inn.

The sunshine had disappeared, and freezing rain dripped through the canopy of trees, creating pools of sucking mud which she hoped would help obliterate the tracks she and Colin left. "What did Sarah say when you told her our plans? Was she angry?"

Colin slowed his steps. "She offered to start the fire herself. She is a brave woman and loyal to my family. However, when my cousin realizes we are not among the inn's guests, he will renew his search for us. They have horses. We do not." He glanced in the direction of the inn. "Riders approach. We have to run." He guided her into the forest and pushed her down behind a fallen tree trunk, pulling brush and leaves over the top of them just as the riders galloped past.

The ground vibrated beneath her like it did with the thunder of an approaching storm. Colin pressed his body near hers, his breathing shallow. Panic rose inside her and seemed to surround her. The only sound was the beat of the horses' hooves as they sped past. When she and Colin were at the inn, she'd heard the men outside, and somehow hearing them joke and carry on a lighthearted conversation was not as frightening as the silence. The men hunting them were angry. They would not fail again.

The riders stopped a short distance away. One of the men barked orders to split up, taking different paths at the fork in the road.

The quiet of the forest returned, and still Colin waited. She followed his lead. This was his world. He would know when it was safe. She ignored the dampness seeping into her clothes from the ground. Better a little discomfort than risk of discovery. Birds chirped somewhere nearby. A squirrel investigated their hiding place, then scampered away.

Colin rose slowly, shedding their cloak of leaves and branches as he sat back on his haunches. "We have to keep moving."

Chapter Twenty-Seven

The village on the edge of the forest looked as though it were sleeping. She'd expected smoke from chimneys, children playing outside, people working in fields, and maybe one of those outdoor markets so popular in Europe. The half dozen or so cottages were dark, their windows and doors shuttered and locked.

Colin had mentioned he would take her someplace safe. The village looked the opposite of safe. There was a haunted tension that smelled of death.

Colin, looking as though he'd felt the ghostlike conditions of the village as well, had gone on ahead and left her here alone with only her imagination to keep her company.

People didn't walk away from their homes unless they had a compelling reason. The first thought she had was the plague. She knew it was airborne and spread like a California wildfire in summer. Any plague outbreaks in the twenty-first century normally occurred in underdeveloped countries. She'd been inoculated against all the standard diseases—measles, mumps, and a litany of others—but was pretty sure the bubonic plague had not been one of them. Wasn't that the disease that turned its victims black, killing them in a matter of days? Survival rate was in the low single digits, and if you did survive, the claim was that your mind and your health were never the same. What would happen if she got sick and died? She'd never return home, and her parents would never know what had happened to her. It was bad enough losing an only child, but to not know what had happened to that child would be worse.

"Stop it," she said aloud. "You're healthy, and you're not going to get the plague." Her imagination had officially taken a side trip to crazy town.

"Why do you believe you will get the Black Death?" Colin said. He knelt beside her, his expression as gray as the morning mist. "Is that what you think happened to the village?" He shook his head and glanced toward the village. "There is a plague, but it is manmade and, thus, far more dangerous."

She reached for his arm and pulled him around. "What do you mean? What happened to the people?"

He kept his back turned away. "One of the old men in the village recognized me and told me the Church's witch hunters arrived a fortnight ago. The men and women of good sense left as soon as they heard the news, packing only what they could carry. Those who remained believed they were not in any danger. According to the old man, those who stayed reasoned that because they feared God, tithed, and attended church on Sunday, they would be safe. Fools, the whole lot of them. The inquisitors know how to turn friends and family against one another. The first victim was murdered this morning—an old woman who had been the village's midwife for over thirty years. She was hanged on the oak tree near the church as a reminder that no one is truly safe."

Madeline shuddered, scanning in the direction he had mentioned. Ravens circled over the church, a few perched on the roofline, and others landed on branches. From her vantage point, she couldn't see the body. She shuddered again. "Why didn't someone in the village defend her against the inquisitors?"

Colin turned slowly around. "Because the villagers were the ones who accused the old woman of witchcraft in the first place. They also accused three others, young midwives and healers, of witchcraft, and then they gathered in the church to demonstrate their piety or hid in their homes. They believed accusing others of witchcraft would draw attention away from themselves. It only condemns them. The inquisitors know how to manipulate hardworking people against anyone, including family and friends. I have seen this before, in my travels to France. Once the witch hunters arrive, whole villages are decimated. The Church will use this village as a warning."

"What will happen to the three women? Will the old man you spoke to help them?"

Colin shook his head. "He is afraid. He said the women are scheduled to die at sunset. Right now, the witch hunters are debating whether they are to die by fire or hanging."

She held her gaze in the direction of the tree where Colin had told her they had hanged the old woman. "My mother would talk about what she called the burning times," Madeline said in a hushed voice, "and the brutal tortures and horrific deaths of thousands of women. How could people be so cruel?" Her voice trembling, she lifted her chin higher. "We have to save the women."

Chapter Twenty-Eight

Colin agreed.

He glanced over toward Madeline as they hid behind a thatch-roofed cottage. Her courage kept surprising him. He had not expected her to want to risk her life to save women accused of witchcraft. Rather than fearing them and what they represented, Madeline's attack had rightfully centered on their accusers, a position he supported.

According to the old man, the accused women were Romani and thus easier to accuse of witchcraft. The women, although skilled healers, had never been fully accepted in the village. According to the villagers, the Romani women had strange ways, liked to dance, and wore colorful clothing and jewelry. Despite the obstacles the women had faced, and in hopes of being accepted, they healed the sick and delivered children, and one of the women had married. In the end, it had not saved them. The villagers had turned on the women the moment the witch hunters had arrived.

The old man's mention that the women were Romani had given Colin an idea. He had sought out this village in search of shelter from Henry and his men. A better place would be a Romani camp. That was, of course, if they were in the area.

He glanced toward Madeline again. She had slipped into a dense clump of bushes, saying she was "going to the toilet," which Colin had learned meant relieving herself of bodily fluids. She had many odd sayings, and perhaps how she talked about her conversation with her mother was another example. Madeline had spoken of her conversations with her mother as though the persecution of witches occurred in the past, not the present.

While he waited for her return, he went over what they had discussed. Their plan was simple. While the witch hunters argued the best way to kill a witch, he and Madeline would unlock the cage where the women were being held. Once the women were freed, the plan was not on quite such firm ground. Few would risk their own lives to harbor women accused of witchcraft. The Church had made examples of people who had offered help to those accused, and condemned them to the same fate. His best hope was if the Romani were in the vicinity.

He had encountered the Romani the second time he ran away, and he'd learned that they were skilled not only in music and the arts but in weaponry as well. They incorporated into their culture the things they learned in their travels and made them uniquely theirs. The Romani were considered mysterious and untrustworthy and were shunned, and his father had forbidden him to seek their company ever again.

Colin had been more careful the next time he visited them.

The underbrush rustled as Madeline came up alongside him. "Are you ready?" The fire in her eyes shone through as though she were rescuing a cherished friend, not perfect strangers.

He nodded, admiring her strength. "Stay close. The

witch hunters are sequestered in the cottage with the red cross painted on the door. When they make their decision, they will head straight for the cage where the women are held prisoner. We can hope to be well on our way by then." He knew he did not need to tell Madeline the consequences if they were discovered trying to rescue the women.

Chapter Twenty-Nine

Madeline didn't think she'd ever been as scared in her life. No matter how much she tried, she couldn't keep from looking in the direction of the tree where the old woman hung. Ravens squawked, and the sound grated against her. She flinched, covering her ears with her hands, and squeezed her eyes shut. It didn't help.

Colin was talking to her, a concerned expression on his face. Had he asked if she'd changed her mind?

"I'm ready," she said in a low whisper, her words muted by the loud beat of her heart.

Clouds deepened the gray day, shutting out the dying rays of the sun as Colin motioned for her to stay close. According to Colin, the cage in the center of the town had been built as soon as the witch hunters had arrived. Their message was clear: they intended to find witches.

The three women in the cage were slumped against each other in silence. Madeline could imagine their protests when the charges were first brought and their reactions when they realized that people they knew had been their accusers. Their glassy-eyed stares reflected both the sting of betrayal and the resignation that they would die. They had lost hope.

Colin reached the cage first and spoke to the nearest woman, whose eyes, the color of coal, reminded him of a rabbit caught in a snare. His hushed words were ignored. She blinked as he raised his voice to gain her attention.

"We will help you escape," he repeated.

The woman next to the black-eyed one peered around her. Her lips were bloodied and the side of her face swollen and bruised. "Why would you help us?"

"It is the right thing to do."

While Colin used his knife to cut through the leather straps binding the door closed, Madeline focused on the woman who'd spoken. A spark of hope rekindled in her eyes. "What is your name?" Madeline asked.

"Molly McCree," said the black-eyed woman. Her voice was hoarse, and her face streaked with tears.

"When the door is unlocked, prepare to run."

Molly put her arm around a younger version of herself. "They broke my sister's leg. I'll not leave her. Take Ann. She is with child, and the father is the one who has condemned her to the witch hunters."

Colin swung the door of the cage wide, holding out his hand. "I will carry your sister. Everyone comes. Now hurry."

Colin reached in for Molly's sister as Madeline kept the door open for Ann and Molly. As soon as they were free of the cage, everyone ran toward the forest. A dog barked, and a flock of birds lifted from a neighboring pine. Either the villagers were too afraid to check on the disturbance outside their doors or they had decided to let the women escape. Madeline prayed it was the latter. She wanted to believe there was still good in people.

They plunged into the dense brush and kept running. Madeline expected to hear shouts and the thunder of horses' hooves at any moment. The path was muddy and uneven, and low-hanging branches scratched her skin and ripped her clothes.

Molly stumbled, and Madeline grabbed her from behind to prevent her from falling.

Colin paused to glance over his shoulder. His hearing was as good as a dog's. She and Molly had barely made a sound. His watchfulness, as though he were their own personal guardian angel, tugged at her heart. Sarah was right. Colin was a good man.

Molly's sister clung to Colin's neck, her face smeared with tears and mud.

Ann leaned against a tree. She panted and held her rounded belly. Ann's slight frame and loose-fitting clothes had hidden the advanced stage of her pregnancy. It was Madeline's guess that stress, fear, and physical exertion were accelerating her labor.

"When is your baby due?" She was hopeful the woman would say in two to three months.

Ann winced as she puffed out shallow breaths. "The babe is coming." Her eyes welled with tears as she doubled over in pain. "She can't come now. It is too soon."

"I know this area," Colin said. "I came here as a child, and I know of a cave a short distance from here. It is small, and the quarters cramped, but it is isolated. There is a chance they might not find us." He looked at Ann. "Do you think you can make it?"

Ann nodded, her cheeks tearstained.

"It is not safe out in the open," Colin said, looking in the direction of the village. "If we can make it into a denser part of the forest, we might have a chance."

"That's what we'll do, then," Madeline said.

"Colin, you carry Ann, and Molly and I will put her sister between us and help her walk."

In silence the switch was made, and they resumed their flight through the woods. Madeline didn't need to be a mind reader to know what was in everyone's thoughts. Even if they made it to the cave there were no guarantees that the witch hunters wouldn't find them. Colin hadn't said how long it would take them to reach the cave. In a way, it didn't matter. They had hope.

Riders leapt out of the forest and headed straight for them. Within a matter of seconds, she, Colin, and the women were surrounded by men on horseback.

Instead of drab, earth-toned tunics over close-fitting leggings, the men wore loose-fitting pants and shirts in vibrant colors. Earrings dangled from their ears, rings covered their fingers, and each brandished a curved sword that gleamed deathly white.

Their clothing was like what Madeline had seen in pictures that depicted the nomadic tribes of European gypsies, or Romani, during the fifteenth and sixteenth centuries. Because the Romani never claimed rights to a country or ruler, their origins were pure speculation. Distrust of a people in Europe who dressed and acted differently ran out of control.

Distrust cut both ways.

Chapter Thirty

Molly screamed with joy and ran toward the horsemen. A rider with a shaved head and a full beard leapt from his horse and rushed to greet her. He swept her into his arms and spun her around.

Colin set Ann down on a fallen tree trunk and remained close. Her face was flushed and her contractions close together. "This woman is in labor," Colin said, "and Molly's sister has a broken leg."

The lead horseman wore an eye patch and sat ramrod straight. A quiet authority surrounded him as he raised his arm in signal to his men. Those in the front row dismounted and ran over to assist Ann and Molly's sister.

The man with the eye patch edged his mount toward Colin. "We are grateful, Colin Penrose, that you rescued our women." His voice held the flavor of exotic spices and faraway lands. "We heard that the witch hunters had invaded the village, and we knew our women would be in danger. We are in your debt. We may not have reached them in time."

"I was glad I could help," Colin said. "I only hope the women's accusers will find justice."

"Be assured that they will, if not in this life, then the next."

Colin folded his arms across his chest and grinned. "When did you grow so formal, Stefan? We are family."

Stefan's face broke out in smiles. "Blame my mother for my formality. She cautioned me that if we should meet again, I should treat you as the son of a lord or suffer the consequences with a cold meal."

"That sounds like Aunty Florica."

The hole in his heart ached. Aunty Florica had told him that she had known his mother, but she had said little else about the woman he never knew. The Romani were a secretive people, and because they moved around so much, he was able to see Aunty Florica only for short periods of time. "How is your mother?"

"Ageless, and I swear it is the result of the brews she blends. My mother will be overjoyed to see you. It has been too long. Come. You will be safe with us."

Chapter Thirty-One

Later that evening, sitting cross-legged on the ground under a canopy of stars, Colin felt at home again, and yet the hole in his heart remained. There were so many unanswered questions. He felt a kinship with the Romani that went beyond his love of their food and music. His mother had been Romani.

His father had let the information slip one day when a group of them had arrived at the castle, seeking an audience. His father refused to speak with them but had sent them away with their wagons filled with food and clothes. When questioned, his father would not discuss the matter. That night, a ten-year-old Colin had run away to the Romani camp and met Stefan.

Colin tipped his bowl of rabbit stew and drained its contents. Stefan sat beside him, leaning against a tree. "How fares the woman with child and the woman with the broken leg?"

"My mother and our healers attended both. The woman with the broken leg is doing well and sleeps as soundly as Ann's babe. Ann gave birth to a healthy girl and named the child after the Lady Madeline." Stefan nudged Colin on the shoulder. "You dance around with your questions, avoiding the one you wish to ask the most. You do not ask me about Madeline. I have never seen you look on a woman as you have on her. How long have you loved her?"

Colin did not challenge how Stefan knew. Stefan was like a brother, and no matter how long between visits, their connection remained strong and unbreakable. "You know me like no other," Colin said. "What you say is true, although this is the first time I have voiced how I feel. Madeline has bewitched me. I cannot hold a thought that will not include her in it."

"I envy you, brother. I long for a woman to bewitch me in that way. There is no greater gift than love. Hold onto her and do not let her go. Where did you find her?"

"In Glastonbury, outside the Thistle Down Inn. Henry was chasing her, and I helped her escape, but not before my cousin tried to kill us both. I thought it strange that he had become so aggressive toward me after all this time."

"Not so strange. Your cousin is in debt and his father threatens to disinherit him. With you dead, the logical choice would be for your father to declare Henry his heir."

Colin gazed out toward the Romani camp. As twilight approached, musicians had gathered, tuning their instruments, while a fresh-killed wild boar roasted over a pit. "If Henry were a better man, and I had confidence he would treat our people with kindness, I would encourage my father to declare him heir."

Stefan glanced toward Colin, then settled his gaze on the camp once more. "A lot of ifs, my friend. Even if Henry were worthy, your father would still have to deal with his brother, Father Patrick. The man is corrupt to his core. If I were to wager, I'd wager that Father Patrick is behind Henry's bloodlust."

"Have you inherited your mother's gift of sight,

that you know what is in their hearts?"

Stefan laughed. "I wish it were so. No, one of my men overheard their conversation at the Thistle Down Inn. The same place you met Madeline."

"It seems our lives are interwoven. Yes, Madeline said she was headed to Tintagel to meet a matchmaker."

"A matchmaker, you say? There's another odd coincidence. We also have a matchmaker. She visits us from time to time and arrived shortly before we headed out to rescue our women."

Stefan motioned over to a gathering by one of the brightly colored wagons with a curved roof.

Colin followed Stefan's gaze. Women from the camp surrounded Madeline and thanked her for helping to save the women from the witch hunters. As though sensing Colin's stare, she glanced over at him and smiled. She laughed and lifted her wrist to show off a half dozen bead bracelets the women had given her.

The impact of her smile knocked the air out of his lungs.

His heartbeat drowned out his surroundings; all he saw was Madeline. He was mesmerized by the way she smiled, the way she tilted her head when she laughed, and the way she tousled the hair on a little girl of about six years of age who asked her a question.

Stefan slapped Colin on the back, jolting him back to earth. "Admit it. You are in love for the first time."

"I cannot love her."

"By the look of your besotted expression, I'd say it is too late. Love cannot be controlled. It is like a breeze and goes where it will."

"Much like the Romani," Colin said, his gaze drifting back toward Madeline. She had turned away and joined others as they gathered around one of the musicians. "You and I know more than most that I cannot love Madeline. I must control how I feel." The women led Madeline toward a curved-roof wagon painted with yellow flowers and scenes of the forest. Panic rose around him. "They are taking Madeline to your mother's wagon."

"Afraid my mother will tell Madeline's fortune and that it will not include you?"

Stefan had guessed his concern. "That might be for the best," he said, feeling as though his voice was choked with smoke. "Whatever future is in store for Madeline, I pray it does not include me."

"Liar."

"My family is cursed," Colin protested.

"Merlin's Curse," Stefan said, with an edge of anger. "How well we Romani remember. We mourn that we could not save your mother from that wicked wizard's curse. You're with us now, and it takes magic to break magic."

"Magic did not save my mother."

"My mother rarely speaks of it, other than to say ignorance was the cause of your mother's death as much as Merlin's Curse and that she believes with all her heart that your mother was a woman out of time."

"If true, it still did not save her." Colin pressed his back against the trunk of the tree. "My father needed Excalibur. Have you made any progress? About a year ago, my men and I dammed Dozmary Pool, searching for the sword, and all we found at its bottom were bones and broken pottery. The last time we met, you had a theory that, instead of lying in Dozmary Pool, Excalibur was secretly stored at the church in

Glastonbury."

"It is no longer a theory. The same man who saw your cousin and his brother at the Thistle Down Inn was there to investigate Father Patrick's claim that he wanted to sell King Arthur's sword. The intent was never to buy the sword, only to verify its authenticity. There is no way to be sure the sword is Arthur's, but the age and description fit the legends. Father Patrick is headed by carriage to Tintagel for the Twelfth Night celebrations. We plan to sneak into the priest's camp while he sleeps, substitute a duplicate sword we had made, and be on our way with no one the wiser. If we leave right away and ride through the night, we will be back before we are missed."

Colin knew Stefan wanted the priest's sword to be Excalibur as much as he did. The Romani had a strong sense of family. Stefan had told him many times that they felt if they had defied Colin's father and stayed in Glastonbury to search for the sword, Colin's mother might not have died.

Although Stefan was certain, there was no guarantee the priest's sword was Excalibur. And if it was, that was only the first step. A woman out of time had to be the person to return it to the Lady of the Lake. Fiona promised she knew of such a person and even now might be waiting at Tintagel with her, expecting Colin to take the woman as his bride.

But could Stefan be right when he said it wasn't a coincidence that Madeline appeared when she did? Was Madeline the woman out of time of whom Fiona spoke?

Laughter floated over to him from Aunty Florica's wagon. He wanted the woman Fiona spoke of to be Madeline. But first, he would need the sword. "Stefan, gather your men. Tonight, we will steal Excalibur and return it to its rightful place."

Chapter Thirty-Two

The interior walls of Aunty Florica's wagon were decorated with murals of meadows and creatures that reminded Madeline of Shakespeare's play *A Midsummer Night's Dream*. Daybeds covered with multi-colored pillows hugged two walls, with a table between. Aunty Florica insisted Madeline exchange her ragged, travel-worn gown for garments like those worn by the Romani.

Whereas the medieval gown was formal and had made her feel like a princess, the gypsy's full skirt, with its jewel-toned colors of saffron, cinnamon, and paprika, brought out her adventurous side and made her feel that anything was possible.

Aunty Florica lit a candle on the table and gestured for Madeline to sit down across from her. "Our clothes look as though they were made for you, child."

"They are so fun. They make me want to learn how to sing, or paint, or twirl in circles until I'm so dizzy I fall down." Madeline stuffed the full-sleeved linen blouse into the waistband of her skirt, shoving on more bracelets as she joined Aunty Florica at the table. "I've never worn so many bracelets in my life. My father disapproved of too much makeup and jewelry, and when I was younger I believed that was the reason why he divorced my mother. When I first started working for him, he insisted I dress conservatively."

147

Aunty Florica shuffled a deck of hand-painted Tarot cards that mirrored the scenes on the walls of the inside and outside of the wagon. "You use many words I do not understand. Is conservative another word for dull?"

Madeline broke out in laughter, thinking of the gray suits and black leather heels that were the uniform of her father's law firm. "Yes, dull is the perfect word to describe how I dressed for work."

"The clothes you wear now suit you better."

"Thank you. They are so much fun to wear. No wonder everyone is always smiling."

Aunty Florica set her card deck aside and handed Madeline a pair of chandelier earrings in hammered silver with bead-like drops of multi-colored stones. "These will suit you as well."

"I can't accept them. Everyone here has already been so generous."

Aunty Florica pushed the earrings into Madeline's hand. "You helped Colin save the lives of three innocents. And I see how much Colin cares for you and you for him. You are part of our family now."

Madeline cradled the earrings in the palm of her hand. They sparkled and caught the candlelight, deepening the silver metal's color and transforming it to shades of gold. Would Aunty Florica and her people change their opinion of her if they knew why she was here? Her reason for traveling back in time was frivolous compared to the life-and-death struggles the Romani faced every day. She handed the earrings back. "You'd change your mind if you knew more about me."

Aunty Florica shook her head. "The earrings are a gift, and as for the rest... I guessed your secret the moment you uttered your first word. I have heard your accent once before."

Madeline's gaze flashed to Aunty Florica's, her pulse racing. Did she know? How could she? Calm down. Granted, her accent was different, but there was no way people could identify it as American. It wasn't as though there was trade between the Americas and Europe. It was fourteen hundred and eight-five, and Columbus didn't reach America until fourteen ninety-two.

Aunty Florica patted Madeline's hand. "You are concerned. Do not be afraid. Your secret is safe with me. Try on the earrings." Aunty Florica dealt out a three-card spread and frowned. "The cards are evasive tonight. They tease me with their mixed messages."

Madeline's fingers quivered as she tried to fasten the earrings. The posts felt too big. Aunty Florica couldn't know. Madeline had traveled through time, and she couldn't explain it, let alone wrap her head around what had happened to her. How could anyone in this century suspect something like that was possible? Maybe Aunty Florica was thinking about something else. Maybe she thought Madeline was married or engaged.

Aunty Florica reached for another deck on the table. This one had hand-painted images of King Arthur and his Knights of the Round Table. She shuffled the cards and, this time dealt a five-card spread. "That is much better," she said, leaning back. "There was a time, long ago, when I met a woman who spoke with an accent like yours. Her name was Catherine Ramírez. She was Colin's mother."

Madeline's pulse spiked, afraid to respond. She

fingered the beads on her bracelet in an effort to remain calm. Aunty Florica had made a connection between her and Colin's mother. But why? Madeline's heart raced. No. That wasn't possible.

The walls of the wagon pressed in around her, and in the murals the forest creature's eyes seemed to focus on her. Her head throbbed. "Colin's mother…"

"Was from the future," Aunty Florica said, finishing Madeline's thought. Aunty Florica tapped a card with the image of a sword, mumbled something to herself, then gathered the cards to shuffle them again. "A matchmaker brought Catherine to me. The matchmaker was a tiny bit of a thing with a touch of the fairies about her. She asked me to say that Catherine was one of my relatives from a Romani tribe to the south."

Aunty Florica had described Nessa. Madeline fingered one of the bracelets on her wrist. "Nessa."

Aunty Florica winked and continued, "Yes, Nessa. My mother told me to always do what a fairy asked of you. The fairies are a cheerful lot but vengeful if they do not get their way. The matchmaker felt certain she could break Merlin's Curse. All went well at first. Colin's father and Catherine were attracted to each other, and as their attraction grew into love, the Romani searched for Excalibur. Their marriage was announced, and all that was left was to find Excalibur."

"As in King Arthur's sword?"

"One and the same. Abruptly, Colin's father ordered the Romani to leave Glastonbury, before they found the sword. We left before the wedding. Ten months later Colin was born, and within an hour of his birth Catherine was dead. Merlin's Curse had murdered again."

Madeline's head pounded, and she rubbed her temples, trying to think clearly. "Wait a second. What are you saying? How is the sword related? It's tragic that Catherine died in childbirth, but that's not so uncommon."

"True. Yet since Merlin placed his curse on the Penrose family, all women who give birth to a Penrose heir die within a week afterward."

"That's creepy."

"Another word from the future. Does it mean tragic?"

"Among other things."

Aunty Florica leaned back against the pillows. "Catherine told me she was from a place called Issaquah, Washington, that was located across the ocean."

Madeline clasped her hands in her lap so tightly her fingers went numb. The old woman spoke gently, yet her words were weighted with questions. "That sounds...that sounds..."

"Like magic," Aunty Florica finished. "I kept her secret, and I will keep yours. Where are you from, child? Because as sure as I am a full-bloodied Romani, it is not from any place I have traveled to in my long years on this earth."

Madeline fidgeted with her beads, rolling them between her fingers. Could she trust this woman?

Aunty Florica shuffled her cards, eyeing Madeline. "Merlin's Curse killed his mother, and that is the reason Colin refuses to marry unless he finds Excalibur. My son has discovered its possible location, and he and Colin leave later tonight to steal it. Colin would rather lose his inheritance than risk a woman's life. Colin is a good man. The matchmaker sent for Catherine because she met the qualifications of 'a woman out of time,' and I believe that same matchmaker brought you here."

The bracelet on Madeline's wrist snapped. Beads bounced to the floor and rolled under the table and beds. This had become complicated really fast. Lady Roselyn hadn't wanted Madeline to go in the first place. Had she known about Catherine and the curse?

She bent down to recover the scattered beads. "You're talking about magic."

Aunty Florica reached down beside Madeline to help pick up the beads. "Magic surrounds you like the halo of light around a star. Do you love Colin?"

Chapter Thirty-Three

Madeline couldn't sleep. Aunty Florica was asleep in the bed on the opposite side of the wagon. Before going to bed, she'd asked Madeline if she loved Colin. That was a complicated question, and as of right now all she could think about was screaming. She had a lot to process. Like Madeline, Colin's mother had been from the future, and somehow Nessa and Excalibur were intertwined in both situations as well.

Outside, Colin and Stefan prepared to leave on their quest to steal Excalibur, and no one had bothered to ask if she wanted to go along. Colin was off on a quest to find the sword, while she was in bed, doing nothing.

Moonlight filtered through the window in Aunty Florica's wagon as the woman snored. Restless, Madeline stared at the painted mural on the ceiling. It depicted a night sky, star constellations, and trails of light from the moon. At first glance, the blue-black sky, with its clusters of white stars appeared peaceful. The longer she stared the more another purpose materialized. A battle raged.

Winged warriors, both men and women, which at first glance had resembled stars, fought in an epic battle. The prize was unclear, and Madeline didn't know her Greek and Roman mythology well enough to know if the scene recreated an ancient battle or was simply a story created from the painter's imagination.

Colin and Stefan's voices grew louder. Aunty Florica's snore rose to match the men's elevated conversation, as though responding, before she mumbled something in her sleep and rolled over. They were behaving as though stealing Excalibur was no big deal. But this was King Arthur's sword. A hundred things could go wrong. How much did Colin really know about the sword? The plan was to steal it. From whom? No doubt whoever had it would have made sure it was well guarded. The fool could get himself killed.

The thought was irrational. Before she arrived, Colin had fought many battles and survived. He didn't need her help.

She focused on a female winged warrior locked in a sword fight with her enemy. Behind her was a wounded comrade she fought to protect.

Madeline squeezed her eyes shut. Just because she had role-played at fairs that she was a knight, and had challenged one of the actors to a sword fight, it didn't mean she was battle ready. Far from it.

She opened her eyes. Then again, Colin and Stefan were after Excalibur. She'd spent her life researching the subject, reading books or watching movies that explained the myths around the sword. Some theories said that Excalibur wasn't pulled from a stone at all. Rather, it had been found in a bog. A recent movie suggested that the Lady of the Lake existed in any body of water, so if you wanted to return the sword to her, all you had to do was fill up a bathtub. The idea received more than a few snorts from the movie's audience. Be that as it may, it confirmed that anything was possible when it came to Excalibur.

In addition, she had the advantage of studying centuries of research, whereas Colin relied on a few handed-down accounts that had been sanitized to reflect the values of the times. He was going into battle with only half the information he needed.

Her father bragged to prospective clients that she rarely lost a case and attributed it to her aggressive demeanor in the courtroom. She'd chafed at the word "aggressive." She wasn't aggressive. She was prepared. She made sure she studied the case backward and forward and made it clear to the client that they needed to divulge all pertinent information. Last but not least, she advised her clients to dress in a professional manner but in a way that didn't shout their wealth and privilege. She needed them to appear sympathetic.

She glanced again at the winged warrior and imagined that she would defeat her enemy and win the day, but not because she was the better swordsman. She would win because she knew her enemy and was better prepared.

Colin may not have asked for her help, but he was going to get it all the same.

Madeline threw off her covers, careful that she didn't wake Aunty Florica as she eased out of bed and gathered her clothes. She crept to the door and mentally fast-forwarded to what her conversation might be like when she told Colin she wanted to go with him. Regardless of how well she argued her case, he was the judge and jury and could prevent her from going along.

She turned the handle on the door. She needed a disguise.

****

The moon had slipped behind the clouds as

Madeline, boots in hand, left the wagon to hide behind clothes hanging on a line. Colin and Stefan were saddling their horses as they waited for others to join them.

She searched through the clothes on the line. Her plan was to wear men's clothing and blend in with the other riders. The items on the line were damp and the pants too big.

"Are we ready to ride, men?" Colin shouted.

She pulled down the smallest pants she could find and slipped them on under her skirt, damp as they were. If he saw her, she could pretend she had come out to say goodbye.

Hiding behind a long blanket hanging to dry, she peered toward Colin. He was mounted and signaling to the other riders.

She needed a horse. A young man was returning from the woods and heading over to his mount. She yanked a cloak off the line, wrapped it around her shoulders, and tugged on her boots as she crept toward him.

The young man hummed as he cinched his saddle.

"Youri," Stefan shouted. "Hurry up, or we'll leave you behind." Stefan reined his horse around and headed in the direction of Colin and the other riders.

Youri said something in Russian as Madeline hit him over the head with a clay pitcher.

Stunned, he rubbed the back of his head and swiveled around. "What the…"

"Sorry," she said and hit him again. The clay pitcher shattered, and Youri crumpled to the ground unconscious.

Madeline shed her skirt, ripped off a ribbon-like

section from it, and tied it around the pants to keep them in place. She mounted the horse and galloped after Colin.

Chapter Thirty-Four

The riders galloped in single file through the forest under a canopy of stars. They had ridden for a little over an hour. The moon hung low in the sky. It was almost dawn. Madeline wrapped the cloak more tightly around her, grateful she'd thought to grab it along with the pants.

The rider in front of her raised his arm as a signal to halt in response to the orders at the front of the line. Madeline pulled the cloak's hood down over her forehead and waited. A campfire glowed through the trees. The rider in front of her raised his arm again, signaling to dismount. No one spoke. Voices carried long distances this late at night, without the usual forest sounds to drown them out.

An owl hooted and another answered in a neighboring tree not far from where Madeline stood next to her horse. Their hunting call broke the silence. Small animals rustled in the underbrush and took off running. The owl hooted again, leapt off its perch, spread its wings, and gave chase.

Another signal from the rider in front of her. This time he motioned to join Colin and Stefan. Leading her horse by its reins, she ducked her head farther under her hood.

Instructions were whispered on each man's role. Their success relied on the element of surprise. The big unknown was where Father Patrick was keeping the sword.

Men peeled off to take their positions, and the rider who had been in front of her during their ride through the forest signaled her to follow him. She shook her head and indicated that her intent was to speak to Colin and Stefan.

The man shook his head, indicating he disagreed, until she rested her hand on the hilt of the knife Colin had given her when they had escaped Sarah's inn. The man shrugged and left to take his assigned post.

Keeping low, Madeline made her way over to Colin and Stefan. They were strategizing on the best time to attack, now or at dawn.

"Did your informant indicate where the sword was hidden?" Colin said.

"Only that he was convinced it was still in Father Patrick's possession. There was a fire in a barn in Glastonbury a few nights ago, and the priest feared it might spread. He didn't want to risk it. Instead of leaving Excalibur in Glastonbury, he brought it with him. We counted eleven of them to our seven. Although our numbers are fewer, we have the element of surprise." Stefan's voice dropped to a level too low for her to hear.

Colin and Stefan might not be concerned that they were outnumbered. She, on the other hand, was plenty worried. The campfire was banked for the night and pulsated an orange-red. The shadows it cast would help hide Colin and Stefan's men when they attacked. At least that was something positive.

Colin glanced over at the camp. "Why would there be three guarded positions? I would assume the priest would keep the sword with him. What need would he have for the other two?"

Stefan raised his head to get a better view. "The priest is clever. Perhaps the three tents are intentional and he means for two of them to be decoys. I'll inform my men that once Excalibur is found, we will leave."

"You can't do that," Madeline said, stepping out from cover.

Colin appeared stunned. "Madeline! What are you doing here?"

She straightened. "Before you get all Mr. Protective on me, I came to help. I think the reason they need to guard three tents is because Excalibur and the scabbard were always kept in separate places until King Arthur went into battle. That accounts for two places, and the third I suspect, is for the priest."

"What are you wearing?" Colin said, and followed up with, "How did you manage to follow us without detection?"

Madeline pulled back. Great. She was in Neanderthal land after all. "I have pants on because riding a horse wearing a long skirt is ludicrous. And I won't get into my opinion of the sexist reason why women are forced to ride sidesaddle. As for following you without detection, that was easy. Everyone was focused on the road ahead, with little thought for the hidden dangers behind them. Which is precisely why I'm here."

Colin towered over her; his body as rigid as the trees at his back. "A woman rides sidesaddle because it is womanly and chaste."

Madeline snorted. "And stupid."

Stefan stepped into the fray. "Keep your voices

down," he said, addressing both Colin and Madeline. "Madeline is here now and offers good advice. We do not need the scabbard, only the sword."

"Actually, that is not true," she said. "In many ways, the scabbard is more important. As long as Arthur wore the scabbard when he fought in battle with Excalibur, it kept his wounds from bleeding or becoming fatal."

"With the new information Madeline provides, we won't need as much time to search after the attack. All will go as planned."

"And if it doesn't?" Colin said, through gritted teeth.

Chapter Thirty-Five

A flock of birds took to the air as one of Stefan's men ran toward him and Colin. The man pointed toward the camp. At least a half dozen riders had joined the priest's men.

Stefan dismissed his soldier. "It's the priest's brother, Henry, and a contingent of the witch hunters who were after you and Madeline. This changes everything. I don't like the odds."

"Neither do I." Colin combed his hands through his hair, glancing from the camp to Madeline and back again. His gaze lingered on hers as he turned toward Stefan. "It is too high a risk. Too many people have already died because of that miserable sword."

"You can't give up now," Madeline said.

The forest stilled as clouds smothered the moon and stars.

"She doesn't know?" Stefan said. "Why didn't you tell her?"

"There was no reason," Colin fought back. "She is not part of this."

Stefan raised an eyebrow. "I would say that the way the two of you look at each other is a strong argument to the contrary."

Madeline moved to stand between the two men. "Would someone please tell me what is going on?"

"Merlin's Curse," both men said at the same time.

Colin rolled his neck as though he struggled with a great weight on his shoulders. "It is the Penrose family curse. Any woman who gives birth to a Penrose heir will die within the first week of doing so. To break the curse we must return Excalibur to the Lady of the Lake and have the heir marry a woman out of time."

She locked on Colin's gaze. There were moments since she'd first met him that she believed he had wanted to kiss her. Something always held him back. A kiss didn't always mean that sex would follow, but it certainly could lead in that direction. Shivers ran down her spine. Was that what she wanted?

"Aunty Florica filled me in," she said, feeling the heat of a blush rise on her face. "That's why I'm here. You need to get that sword."

"You keep surprising me." Colin broke her gaze as though it gave him pain. "I agree. But now is not the time."

"Wait a minute," Madeline said. "There has to be another way to get the sword, something that doesn't involve attacking the camp."

Colin's eyes widened. "Of course! Stefan, you mentioned that one of your men had offered to buy the sword from Father Patrick in Glastonbury."

"Yes, but the priest's price was too exorbitant," Stefan said. "Our intention was always to steal it when we had the opportunity."

"I will gladly reimburse you, regardless of the cost."

Stefan nodded slowly. "It might work. Father Patrick is aware that the man he dealt with is Romani. One of my men can present a new offer. I'll make the necessary arrangements."

Chapter Thirty-Six

Colin lay on his stomach beneath the cover of low-hanging tree branches. The negotiations in the camp were under way. He did not need to have the ability of a Romani fortuneteller to figure out how they were going. Father Patrick refused to sell the scabbard along with the sword.

They needed a new plan.

A crowd had gathered around Father Patrick and the negotiator. The negotiator insisted his price was for both sword and scabbard.

"You need my help." Madeline edged in next to Colin under the branches and pulled leaves out of her long curls.

She was covered in trail dust and mud; leaves and twigs littered her hair, and yet she was the most beautiful woman he had ever seen. "Absolutely not."

She nudged him on the shoulder. "If it weren't for me, we'd be on our way back to the Romani camp empty-handed. I can help. Stefan positioned all of his men as a show of strength around the negotiator and Father Patrick. That leaves you and Stefan with three places to search. I can help. How long do you think it will be before the priest changes his mind?"

"Why are you doing this?" Colin said. "This is not your problem."

She leaned in closer until their noses almost

touched. "Maybe I don't like how this curse has ruined so many lives, or maybe it's as simple as me wanting to see what's it's like to kiss you, and I know you won't even try while this curse thing hangs over your head. Either way, I'm taking the tent farthest from the fire. That leaves the other two for you and Stefan. I'll meet you back here."

She left him with his mouth gaping open. How did she know that he yearned to kiss her? Extraordinary woman. His father said women were a mystery, and now Colin understood what he meant. He shook free of the thought of her lips on his as he made his way over to Stefan to tell him of the new plan, all the while keeping track of Madeline's progress. The man guarding the tent she had headed toward was paying more attention to the negotiations than to his duties.

So far so good.

****

Only when Madeline emerged from the tent with something tucked under her cloak and reached the safety of Stefan's men did Colin make a move toward the tent he was to search. Stefan was next to his and disappeared inside. Colin sighed in relief and caught Madeline's glance as she made her way to their rendezvous point. She peeled back her cloak enough so that steel glinted in the moon's light. She had the sword.

He waited a few more heartbeats until he knew she was clear of the camp before he moved toward the tent he was to search. Stefan was still searching his as Colin slipped past the guard and crawled under the back of the tent. For this to work, they must escape before the priest ended the negotiations.

The inside of the tent was sparse. A leather-bound Bible lay on top of folded bedding in one corner, with a wooden crate placed next to the tent's opening. The logical choice was the crate. It was near the entrance and in full view of the guard. This looked like Father Patrick's quarters, and if he was like his brother Henry, logic never entered into a decision. They operated on pure emotion. If they wanted something, they took it.

Madeline had said the scabbard protected a person in battle by preventing wounds from bleeding. The priest would want something like that as close to him as possible. He might even believe the scabbard would make him invincible.

Men's voices raised. The priest was agitated, but so was the negotiator.

Colin needed to hurry. He bent to the task of unrolling the bedding. The scabbard lay near the bottom. Symbols were burned into the weathered leather, and small needle holes holding bits of faded threads hinted at the embroidery Guinevere was supposed to have done on it. He grabbed the scabbard, replaced the bedding and Bible, and retreated the way he had entered.

With the scabbard hidden under his jacket, Colin raced to the rendezvous location. Madeline and Stefan were waiting for him.

"Do you have it?" Stefan asked. With a nod from Colin, Stefan rushed on, "I sent word to the negotiator to give us a few more minutes and then end it with the priest. We want to be long gone before they discover we stole the sword and its scabbard."

Chapter Thirty-Seven

The next evening, stringed instruments joined the celebration as people gathered around the Romani campfires. The discovery of Excalibur fueled the good mood. Flames swayed in the gentle wind in rhythm with the movement of the dancers. Madeline clapped along with the others standing around the circle.

The bright, jewel-toned clothing and the warmth of the fire chased away the winter gloom. The forest clearing had been transformed into an enchanted glen, a place out of time. Tables were set up with breads and pierogi noodle pudding with dried fruits and butter, while bubbling stews of rabbit and hedgehog, combined with spices and root vegetables, simmered over the fire. The atmosphere, surreal in its calmness and joy, spread over everyone like an enchanted breeze.

Was that how Colin's mother had felt when she'd first arrived at the Romani camp? It must have seemed romantic. And then Catherine had met Colin's father, who, from what Aunty Florica had said, had swept her off her feet. Had Colin's father felt the same? Had he told Catherine about the curse or kept it a secret?

Sparks of light danced in the firepit like hundreds of fairies caught in the merriment. She knew it was her imagination. There was no such thing as fairies, but even the thought of them promised that anything was possible, even a magical happily-ever-after ending.

A burst of children's laughter exploded nearby. They had tackled Colin to the ground and were showering him with sugary berry desserts. Colin formed his hands to resemble claws and roared like a bear. The children giggled and scampered back, chanting, "Dragon. Dragon. Dragon."

Free of the pile of children and covered in dripping berry juice, Colin stood. He wore a red cape and a helmet shaped like the head of a dragon. He was magnificent. Madeline couldn't look away.

The children's giggles and laughter gained momentum. Some squealed; others shouted with glee. Their excitement was contagious. A few adults wandered over to see the big attraction.

"The children have taken a liking to your man," a petite young woman said. Her dress was created from layers of multicolored silks in purple, sunflower yellow, and daisy white. The tips of her spiky blonde hair looked like they had been dipped in eggshell-blue paint. She added, "Colin will make a good father one day."

"Colin and I are not…"

Madeline's comment caught in midsentence. "Wait! I remember you. You're Nessa. You're the one who pushed me over the threshold. You look different somehow."

"As do you. It's this place. It brings out our true selves."

"Lady Roselyn didn't want me to go, did she?"

Nessa tucked her hair behind her slightly pointed ears. "My sister doesn't understand."

Three little girls around the ages of six or seven skipped in the direction of Madeline, and as they passed Nessa, they each touched their ears and then pointed at

Nessa's and giggled and waved.

Nessa touched her ears as well and winked. The children broke into peals of laughter as they skipped past Nessa on their way to the food table.

"Children love you," Madeline said, with a twinge of something she couldn't identify. Was it regret?

"Children love you as well. Open your heart."

"It's not that easy."

"Time will tell. Did you like your fortune? Aunty Florica is one of the Romani's best fortunetellers and healers. She heals both the body and the heart."

Madeline stopped short of asking the young woman how she knew. This was a small camp, so no doubt there weren't any secrets. "Aunty Florica said the usual things, that the way to find love is to love yourself and to not be afraid to take a leap. As for the rest, I'm not sure I believe in magic."

"You also didn't believe in time travel before you arrived here." Nessa picked a palm-sized pinecone from the ground and peeled off a few of its scale-like layers. She popped one of them into her mouth and crunched it like a nut. "Would you like one? They are delicious this time of year."

Madeline shook her head and tamped down the impulse to ask Nessa if pinecones were fairy food. "Aunty Florica said you brought Colin's mother here from the future."

Nessa nodded and popped another piece of pinecone into her mouth. "It should have worked. This time will be different. Colin is not as closed off as his father, and thanks to you, he has Excalibur. The two of you were meant to be together."

"You are talking about together forever after.

Everything is happening too fast. I came here to find a date for my mother's wedding. I'm the slow-and-steady type, not the jump-and-hope-a-net-appears type. Remember, I didn't walk over the threshold—you pushed me. Maybe your being here is a sign I should return before I get in any deeper."

Nessa tossed the pinecone into the woods. "If that is your wish, we can leave right now. But ask yourself this: do you *want* to leave just when things between you and Colin are getting interesting?"

Chapter Thirty-Eight

Madeline glanced over at Colin as Nessa's words sank in. Did she want to leave him?

On the far side of the camp, Colin was in the middle of a circle of children engaged in a mock battle with a young boy as his friends clapped and cheered. Colin's expression was relaxed and open. She had never seen him this happy. Was Nessa right? Madeline was just getting to know Colin.

What was so wrong with staying a few more days? She could ask Colin if he'd like to be her date for her mother's wedding, although of course that would involve telling him she was from the future. How would she start her confession? Should she tell him his mother was from the future, as a lead-in to say she was as well? Was this something where you eased into it, or ripped off the bandage? Would he think she was losing her mind? Did they have insane asylums in the fifteenth century?

She was doing it again. She was overthinking the issue. Overthinking worked when you prepared for a case. This was different.

The whole reason for going back in time had been to find a date for her mother's wedding.

"You're right, Nessa. I'll stay a little longer. Could you get a message to my mother? Tell her I'm fine and plan to return in time for her wedding." When Nessa didn't respond, Madeline turned the direction she'd last seen her.

Nessa had vanished as suddenly as she had appeared.

Had Nessa known that Madeline would want to stay?

Colin's deep-throated roar rose over the camp, followed by children's laughter and cheers. Instead of a dragon, Colin now played the role of a bear. He lumbered after the children in a mock chase, roared again, and bared his teeth.

A boy with a mane of curly black hair thrust his toy sword at the bear's chest. Colin feigned injury and made a dramatic crash to the ground, complete with loud groans and flapping arms.

"Madeline, help!" Colin shouted. His voice was laced with laughter.

The children had piled on top of him again. His face and beard were covered in gooey berry juice.

Madeline laughed and hurried to his rescue. As she ran, her earrings tinkled like wind chimes against her neck, making her feel like magic was in the air. She'd grown up an only child, and although her parents told her that meant she had their undivided attention, she had longed for brothers and sisters. The Romani had welcomed her with open arms, reminding her of those childhood dreams.

She reached the pile of children and gently lifted them away from Colin. "Let's give the bear a rest, shall we?" When they resisted, she pretended to sniff the air. "I smell a fresh batch of sweets over by the cook wagon."

The boy who'd wielded the wooden sword also

sniffed the air. He raised his weapon and shouted his delight as he led the charge in the direction she'd indicated.

The children chased after him, except for the little girl who'd given her a bracelet when she first arrived. The child handed Madeline another bracelet, this one made of small, polished amber stones, then rushed to catch up with her friends.

Shivers of delight sped over Madeline's arms, and her vision blurred. Adding the bracelet to the growing collection on her wrist, she looked for the child. The little girl had melted into the crowd gathered around the cook wagon. A warm wave washed over her at the child's kind gesture. How could she have thought, even for a second, that she didn't want to have children? She wanted lots of them. She wanted her house filled with their laughter.

She covered her hand over the bracelets. The two the child had given her were made of amber. The three with multi-colored stones were from Molly and her sister in gratitude for helping rescue them. The white stone bracelet was from Ann, the third woman she and Colin had rescued, and the red stone one was a gift from Aunty Florica. Seven in total, their worth was more priceless to Madeline than diamonds and gold.

She blinked away a tear as she turned toward Colin.

Colin dusted off his clothes and was picking berries and chunks of sweet pastries out of his beard. "Thank you." He smiled. "Playing with children is exhausting, but a lot of fun."

"Well, there were ten of the little warriors and only one of you." She swiped at her eyes and then brushed berries and sugary crumbs off his shoulder, feeling the cords of muscles beneath his shirt. Her hand lingered on his chest. "You were really patient with them." She cleared her throat, remembering that Nessa had said she thought Colin would make a good father. "We should get you cleaned up."

"If you are suggesting a bath, I already bathed."

She crossed her arms over her chest. "Dunking your head into a horse trough does not count."

He lifted her hand, brushed his lips over her skin, then raised his gaze. "I bathed in the river near camp right after we arrived this morning."

A vision of Colin's naked body sent parts of her tingling as other parts awoke to new possibilities. "You were naked?" She clamped her mouth shut. "I mean, did you use soap?"

He licked juice off the side of his mouth with his tongue. "Yes, I used soap, but alas I'm in need of another bath. Would you like to walk with me to the river and help me clean off the berry juice?"

Her skin flushed under his stare. "I would like that very much."

He kissed the back of her hand again. "Then I am all yours."

Chapter Thirty-Nine

It had taken longer to reach the river than expected. Colin was stopped every few feet by well-wishers congratulating him on finding Excalibur.

Madeline took in each conversation, noting the sense of relief and pride that people expressed. It was as though a weight had been lifted, not only from Colin but from the Romani tribe also. There was a lightness to Colin's step and a more boyish tone to his voice. At one point, one of the men had slipped into a language that sounded like Hindi, and Colin had responded in the same language.

Stars dusted the night sky in silver light, with the moon as its pearl-like jewel. Madeline laid a blanket on the ground and suggested that Colin dunk his head in the water to clean off the berry juice. She sat on the blanket and drew her legs to her chest.

Colin had removed his jacket and shirt and trimmed his hair and beard. His broad shoulders and back flexed as he scrubbed his face with soap. She tried to concentrate on anywhere but his naked chest—and failed. When she'd first seen him in the barn in Glastonbury, even before she realized it was the man that she'd met last year, she wondered what he would look like if he were clean shaven. Her father said you couldn't trust a man who wore a beard.

Like everything else in her life until now, she had

shared her father's opinion. It was easier. Less conflict. Now all she could think about was how her blood quickened when she thought about how Colin's beard would feel against her skin. "Why did you decide to trim your beard? You're not going to shave it all off, are you?" Her face flushed. She pulled her legs tighter against her chest. It shouldn't matter.

He ran his hand over his beard. "That depends. But to answer your question, Aunty Florica scolded me on my appearance. She is the one who handed me the soap and said if I wanted a woman to kiss me, I had better make myself more desirable."

Heat flashed around her neck and rose higher. "Aunty Florica actually used that word?" Madeline held her breath. "You want a woman to kiss you?"

"That depends." Starlight glinted in his eyes and they turned silver, a shade filled with magic.

"You keep using that expression," Madeline said. "It depends on what?"

"It depends on you." He ducked his head under the water again as though his words hadn't turned her world upside down.

Madeline's mouth gaped open. She shut it so fast her teeth shuddered. Was he saying he wanted to kiss her? Did she want him to? Duh! She felt as nervous as a schoolgirl on her first date. Should she wait for him to kiss her, or should she make the first move? He was joking with her. Just casual flirting, nothing more. Or was it foreplay?

He yanked his head out of the water and shook it, spraying her with water.

She laughed, releasing the tension that had built up inside, and held up a drying towel. "You're getting me all wet." Her hands trembled as she stood and handed him the cloth to dry his face.

His smile was mischievous. "Maybe that was my intent."

Her skin flushed until she thought the heat would consume her. Oh. My. God. She couldn't breathe. She sank onto the blanket-covered ground and almost lost her balance. It was not her most graceful move.

He was beside her on the blanket, taking her hand in his and asking if she was all right. Warm waves rolled off his chest and shoulders like heat from a fire. Why was he still half naked? She should demand that he put on a shirt.

"I'm okay," she said resisting the urge to kiss him. "I must have tripped over a rock or twig or something." She picked up the cloth he'd used to dry his face. It was still damp. She pressed it against her face to cool her flushed skin. "The children loved playing with you," she said, focusing on a safe topic. "They looked like they were having so much fun."

"It was I who I think had the more fun. It has been a long time since I laughed that much." He leaned back on his elbows. "Children need time to laugh and play. More so, if they are left orphaned. One day I plan to build an orphanage and give strict instructions that the only thing children are to do all day is laugh and play."

"What about school?" she asked with a smile. "They should learn how to read and write."

"I concede to your suggestion," he said in mock seriousness. "But only if lessons are every other day. Children should have time to be themselves and explore. Too often they are expected to take on adult tasks as soon as they can walk. It is not right."

She stretched out on her side beside him. It was so easy to be around him, as though she'd known him most of her life. How could a man from the past connect with her in such a deep way? She propped on her elbow, head in her hand, and met his gaze. "It's obvious that you love children. Me too. Do you think it's because you never had any sisters or brothers? I know that's why I want children."

He brushed hair off her forehead, his touch feather-soft. "How many children would you like to have?"

"Tonight, while watching you play with the children, I decided I'd want to have at least a dozen. When I'm thinking more realistically, three or four. How about you?"

He lay on his back with his arms behind his head. "I would like enough children to fill a castle with laughter. You said you did not have any sisters or brothers. Did your mother also die when you were young?"

She had a strong feeling that her mother would love Colin. "No, my mother is very much alive, with plans to marry soon."

"I am sorry—not that your mother will remarry, but because it means your father died."

She lay on her back and studied the stars. They blinked in and out as though winking at the mortals below. Judge away, she wanted to tell them. Tonight was a night for new beginnings. "My father is alive and well. He left my mother when I was six years old." The old pang of abandonment flared in her chest, feeling as though it might suffocate her. She swallowed and pushed it back down.

He turned his head toward her. "How could a man

leave a woman he pledged to love and cherish, especially one who has given him a child? There is no greater gift than children."

The sincerity and force of his declaration glowed as clear and passionate as the stars. Take a leap, her heart whispered.

Chapter Forty

Madeline felt time slow.

Snowflakes reflected the moon's glow and floated on the air currents. They swirled and danced like hundreds of pinpoints of light. Colin removed a snowflake from Madeline's hair, and it melted on his warm fingers.

His hand lingered on her shoulder. "Do you want to go inside?" His voice was thick with desire.

She leaned closer, her lips touching his as she whispered against his mouth, "Not yet."

The passion shone in his eyes as his lips parted. The intensity of his kiss matched hers. Her senses came alive. An owl announced its presence, a fish broke the surface of the water, and a breeze chased the scent of pine and fir in her direction. This was real. Colin was real.

Love broke free.

How long had she loved him? Was that the real reason she'd given in to Gran's suggestion that Madeline invite Colin to the wedding? It was the excuse she needed. She wanted to find him. It had nothing to do with a date for her mother's wedding.

She intensified the kiss, guiding Colin toward her as he pulled the blanket over them and the world fell away.

Chapter Forty-One

The Romani had buttoned up for the night. Children were tucked in bed, the food and tables put away, and the fires banked for the night. Guards patrolled the grounds and men and women took turns tending the fire throughout the night. The message was clear. If they needed to leave in a hurry, all they would have to do is hitch the horses to the wagons. They were a nomadic tribe, distrusted and feared because they were different. Without warning, and sometimes without cause, other people might attack and try to drive them away. They had to be ready.

When they reached the wagon she shared with Aunty Florica, Madeline took the blanket from Colin's arms.

"Madeline..." He closed his eyes, and when he opened them, he said, "If you were mine, I would never leave you."

The words were impossible. Merlin's Curse stood between them and made her feel as though a cloud hovered over them. She knew he meant every word. She also held onto too many secrets for Colin's words to become reality. What would he think if he knew she was from the future and had come here with the silly idea of searching for a date while he battled issues that had real-life consequences?

Making her decision, she let the blanket fall to her

feet. She leaned up until his mouth was a breath away from hers, his eyes clear and honest in the starlight. Her life in the twenty-first century was the dream. This was the reality she wanted to live.

Repeating the words he'd spoken, she said, "If you were mine, I would never leave you."

Colin's arms wrapped around her waist, crushing her against him. His mouth heated hers, and the world disappeared.

****

Madeline woke with a smile on her face and to a knock on the wagon's door. She smiled again, touching her fingers to her mouth, so well loved by Colin's kisses last night. "I'm awake. Just give me a few minutes." Last night had been magical. She laughed at the use of the word. Nessa was right…again. Madeline did believe in magic.

She stretched, feeling guilty that she'd overslept. Aunty Florica's bed was vacant. No doubt she had been up for hours, helping to prepare breakfast.

Madeline threw off the quilt and got out of bed, reaching for her clothes. Aunty Florica had laid out the ones she'd given Madeline, as well as the ones Madeline had worn when she arrived in this century. She chose the clothes Aunty Florica had given her.

She slipped on the bracelets with special care to position the ones the little girl had given her. "I'm ready and starving," she said, opening the door. Colin was waiting for her as though he had come to wake her. "Do you think there's any of that beautiful bread left…" Her words died on the wind.

The campsite was swept clean, and a nervous energy charged the air. Horses were hitched to wagons, cookfires extinguished, and their embers beaten to ash. Children were inside wagons, while the adults prepared to leave.

"Why is everyone leaving?"

Colin offered his hand to help her down the wagon's wooden stairs. "Stefan does not want to take any chances that Father Patrick and his men might suspect it was the Romani who stole the sword and its scabbard, especially since they have joined forces with the witch hunters. The Romani travel to the north, while we will journey by carriage to my castle by way of Dozmary Pool."

"That's one of the places where the Lady of the Lake lives." She sucked in her breath. "You plan to return the sword today. But wouldn't a horse be faster?"

He kissed the back of her hand. "Much faster. But with you beside me, I would prefer to go slow."

Chapter Forty-Two

Mist rolled over Dozmary Pool like clouds drifting over a summer's sky. According to Colin, they were only about nineteen miles from his island castle. Madeline sat on a fallen log as Colin unwrapped what they hoped was Excalibur in its scabbard. There was really no way to know for sure without testing it. Legend claimed that the blade glowed so bright it blinded King Arthur's enemies, but using such a powerful weapon was dangerous.

She took a furtive glance toward their driver, an old man with rounded shoulders and a slight limp. The man had unhitched the horses and let them graze on a tether while he dozed.

"Does our driver know what we're doing? Can you trust him?"

"Gregor is like a second father to me. He and his wife and family made me feel welcome when I ran away from home. I would trust him with my life. I am anxious to see what this sword looks like." He finished the unwrapping and laid the sword and scabbard on the ground.

Colin withdrew the battle sword from its scabbard. The blade was unremarkable. Years of neglect had left its mark. The hilt was wrapped in leather strips, stained dark from battles won and lost. The guard and blade were chipped and dull from lack of care. Nothing distinguished it save a simple moonstone at the base of the guard. The milky-white stone lay dormant, waiting for Arthur's return.

Madeline reached out to touch the moonstone. She'd read countless books about the legend, and always in the back of her mind she'd considered it a great story but just that—a story—until now. Her fingers trembled as she pulled back her hand. She wanted the stories to be real.

She rubbed her fingers over the hilt of the blade and half expected it to be warm to the touch. When it wasn't, she drew back her hand, disappointed. "The storytellers say that the real magic of the sword was that King Arthur believed in its power to unite his kingdom. At the end of his reign he'd lost Guinevere, and it was becoming harder and harder for him to keep the balance in his land. Then Excalibur was stolen. When he faced his son Mordred in battle, the sword King Arthur wielded broke in half. It was then that he realized Mordred had his sword. Soon after, Mordred dealt Arthur a mortal blow."

"What if this is not the true sword of Arthur Pendragon?" Colin said.

"We won't know until we see if the Lady of the Lake accepts it back," Madeline said. "Legend says that if you throw Excalibur into a body of water, the Lady of the Lake will rise and retrieve it. Dozmary Pool is one of the locations where legends claim Merlin returned the sword to her. What have we got to lose? You should throw it into the water and see what happens."

Colin handed the sword to Madeline. "According to the curse, only a woman can return it."

With reverence, Madeline accepted it from Colin

and walked to the edge of the pool. The blade was lighter than she'd expected. She drew it over her head and threw it into the air. It arced over the water and cut its way through the mist. The mist thickened as she followed it with the scabbard.

She waited for a splash. None came.

Ripples spread over the water and waves caressed the shoreline.

"That was strange," Madeline said. "Did you see or hear anything?"

"For a moment I thought I saw..." He turned away from the shore. "This is madness. The sword belonged to a forgotten warrior, nothing more. Merlin's Curse will never be broken."

The waves quieted, and the mist lifted from the glass-smooth water. The moon shone in the center of the pool, reflecting the same shade as the moonstone on the hilt of the sword. Clouds moved across the moon as a breeze rippled over the water.

Suddenly, the moon disappeared as though by magic.

Madeline felt an odd sense of calm, as though she'd received a message. "I disagree. I have faith that we have returned Excalibur to the Lady of the Lake."

Colin's lips gently touched hers. "One day I pray I have faith as strong as yours."

The sky opened, and snow drifted down in fluffy, soft flakes like bits of lace, melting on Madeline's hand and decorating her clothes. "I don't want to leave." She had meant Dozmary Pool, but once the words were spoken, she knew she meant that she didn't want to leave Colin. Her heart wanted to stay with him. The logical side of her argued that it was time to leave before she got in any deeper.

Colin stood, dusted off his tunic, and reached for her hand. "We will take our time. Our carriage awaits, milady."

Once inside the carriage, Madeline and Colin sat on opposite sides as Gregor spread blankets over them, closed the door, and climbed onto the driver's bench. A snap of the reins and the carriage lurched forward.

Madeline fell forward into Colin's arms.

He laughed softly and kissed her hair, pulling her close. "I wanted you in my arms the moment we first met."

"And I thought you were the most beautiful beast I had ever seen in my life."

"A beast?"

She tugged on his beard. "I said beautiful."

"So you did," he said, kissing her on her nose. He took her face in his hands. "When I first saw you, you were helping your grandmother. The next you were fighting off Henry and his men. I thought you both kind and...what was that word you used to describe Aunty Florica?"

"Fierce."

He kissed her lips. "Fierce."

The carriage rolled over an uneven section of the road and jolted Madeline against Colin. She threaded her hands behind his neck as the carriage smoothed out its tempo over the road. Colin pulled the blanket around them, kissing the nape of her neck, his hand spreading over the small of her back.

She was on fire from within as each kiss fueled the flames higher. He kissed her behind her ear. His breath sent shivers of desire racing over her heated skin.

"I love you," Colin whispered.

"I love you too," Madeline said, kissing him with all the passion in her heart.

"Marry me on Christmas Eve," he said, pulling away enough to look in her eyes.

There were a hundred reasons she should say no.

Her lips parted, and she pulled him against her. "Yes," she said against his mouth.

The gentle sway of the carriage created a world unto itself, a cocoon of magic and infinite possibilities. She had told him she loved him. The words didn't feel big enough for what she felt. He wasn't a perfect man, but he was perfect for her.

Chapter Forty-Three

Madeline rested in Colin's arms, basking in the afterglow of their lovemaking. She'd told him she loved him and promised to marry him, yet a big secret hung over her like a dark cloud. She hadn't told him that she was from the future. How would he react? Plus, what about her parents…and Gran? If she stayed, she would never see them again. Would she be okay with that decision?

Colin kissed the top of her head, stroking her arm. "You are deep in thought, my dearest."

"I was thinking about my family."

"Would you like to invite them to our wedding?"

She wondered if it would be possible. She nuzzled against his chest, comforted by the steady beat of his heart. "Christmas Eve is in only a couple of days, and my family lives a long way away." The irony was that although Glastonbury was only about a hundred twenty miles from Tintagel, her family wouldn't be there for at least six hundred years.

Gregor rapped on the side of the carriage. "We're under attack." He snapped the reins, and the carriage lurched forward.

Madeline took the seat opposite Colin and braced her hands against the sides of the carriage.

Colin disentangled from the blankets. "I am going to help Gregor drive. Slide farther over. I have to open the door."

Madeline reached for his arm. "Are you crazy? You can't climb out of a moving carriage. You'll kill yourself."

The carriage lurched again, bucking Madeline to the space between the bench seats.

Colin helped her settle back in place. "Hold onto the leather straps tied to the sides. I will be back."

"That's what an action hero in a movie always says," Madeline said under her breath.

"What is an action hero?"

She shook her head. "Not important. Just be careful. Don't get dead. I just told you I love you."

He grinned. "You told me many times, actually."

She clung to the straps and shook her head. "Just go. And remember to keep your promise."

Colin opened the door and climbed out of the carriage. The door gaped open, swinging back and forth on its hinges. As the carriage sped at breakneck speed down the road toward Tintagel Castle, horsemen exploded from the surrounding forest.

The rider in the lead yelled, "Give us the sword, and we will let you live."

She heard Colin shout to the horses to run faster and snapped the reins. The carriage tilted to the side as it raced around a curve. Madeline held on, leaning with the carriage. She recognized her surroundings. A tree scorched by fire. A small thatch-roofed cottage. They were getting close. The only problem was that Tintagel Castle was on an island. If the boat wasn't docked, they'd have to stand and fight.

Chapter Forty-Four

A brisk wind drove the waves against the cliffs of Tintagel Castle, sending a salt-sea spray into the late afternoon air as Fiona walked along the path. She flipped her hood over her hair and kept walking, pounding out her frustration. It had been days, and still no word about Colin and Madeline.

She knew Nessa wanted this match to work out, and it wasn't that Fiona didn't share her view. It was just that she was worried for Madeline, and she had a terrible premonition that those who sought the sword wouldn't stop until they recovered it again. What was Nessa thinking when she planned this match a year ago?

Then, on top of everything else, Liam had left before dawn to investigate a stolen document in Trinity College in Dublin. He wouldn't share the details, and she was so upset with him for leaving that all she could do was stomp away without saying goodbye. And of course she felt guilty. She'd deal with him when he returned. Right now, she had more pressing issues.

She needed to confront her half-sister. The servants had told her that Nessa had arrived late last night, and Fiona knew exactly where to find her. She spotted her at the edge of an outcropping of rocks, feeding the birds. The area had a clear view of the dock on the other side of the narrow slip of water that separated

Tintagel Island from the mainland. Nessa was surrounded by several hungry seagulls.

Fiona strolled over to her, and as she did, the seagulls lifted into the air and flew to a neighboring cliff. She swept her half-sister into a warm embrace and realized Nessa was skin and bones beneath the layers of clothing, and there were dark circles under her eyes. All the angry words Fiona had wanted to say evaporated on the wind. Nessa was as worried as she was.

"I'm so glad to see you." And she meant it. "Why are you here, though?"

Nessa's scarlet cape gently lifted and flapped behind her like wings. "I had to fix things. You shouldn't be out in this weather. The baby doesn't like the wind. It gives her hiccups."

Fiona rubbed her belly as she eyed Nessa. Nessa knew she was pregnant and that the baby didn't like the wind. Fiona and her sisters were still getting used to Nessa's ways of knowing things she shouldn't. The young woman was a mystery. She had dropped into their lives without warning, as though she'd known she was needed, and they were still puzzled by her in many ways.

Fiona pulled her cloak tighter to protect her baby from the wind. "I'm worried about this match."

"Well, it's a good thing there are two of us here so we can make sure that love wins."

"We might not win this one," Fiona said. "Merlin's Curse could keep Madeline and Colin apart. Aunty Florica told me about Catherine. You can't wish that same fate on Madeline."

A lone seagull landed beside Nessa's feet. She reached into a cloth bag attached at her waist and bent down to feed the bird a few seeds. "Madeline and Colin returned Excalibur and the scabbard to Dozmary Pool."

Fiona sucked in her breath. "Then they must believe the sword is real." She peered toward the mainland. "Shouldn't they have returned here by now?"

Nessa's laughter was as light as the flap of butterfly wings. "Dozmary Pool is a magical place. Give them time. Wondrous things happen there."

"Did you send Colin's parents there as well? I'm aware that you orchestrated the match between Catherine and Colin's father."

A cloud darkened Nessa's expression. "They never had the opportunity to return the sword, but yes, I was responsible for their meeting." She stroked the seagull on the head. It trilled and leaned against her hand. "Catherine and John fell in love at first sight, and a wedding date was set. I told the Romani that Excalibur was hidden in the church of Glastonbury. I wished I could have stolen the sword myself. It would have been so much easier. It is a magical blade, forged on the Isle of Avalon, and I am forbidden to touch it, much to my deepest regret. I truly believed that everything was in place. Catherine and John were in love, and the Romani were poised to find the sword. Then an old priest told John the Romani were not to be trusted and that he must send them away."

"You didn't count on the power of superstition," Fiona said.

"No, I did not, and I should have known better." The seagull took flight, winging its way to join its friends. Nessa straightened and dusted off her hands. "This time will be different."

Fiona put her arm around Nessa's shoulders. When

Nessa had first arrived, Fiona had had her doubts about the young woman who was her mother's long-lost daughter by a man no one had met. Fiona, Bridget, and Lady Roselyn had doubted Nessa possessed matchmaking skills, as they knew so little about her. An important quality in a matchmaker was the belief that love was the strongest emotion. Fiona hadn't discovered much more about Nessa since the first day they'd met, but she was sure about one thing. Nessa was a matchmaker.

"You planned the whole thing from the beginning. A year ago, you sent Colin to the future to meet Madeline. For some reason, it didn't work out, so you decided to give Colin and Madeline a second chance. How did you get Madeline to want to go back in time and search for Colin?"

Nessa's laugh returned. "Madeline's grandmother and I had a little chat. It seems she believes in…well, people like me. She had met Colin and liked him. She's the one who insisted Madeline bring Colin to the wedding. You know the rest."

"That's why you did something to the door here at Tintagel. You wanted Madeline to come to him, and you wanted them on a journey together."

"Madeline is a match for Colin. I could feel it the moment I met her. What better way to get to know each other and fall in love than on a quest? Now that the sword is returned, all that is left is for them to admit that they are meant to be together," said Nessa.

"I hate to state the obvious, but what if the sword isn't Excalibur?" Fiona stood up straighter. "Did you hear something?" She moved closer to the edge of the cliff, straining to get a better view of the mainland.

She'd heard shouting. Just then, a carriage sped into the clearing, chased by horsemen brandishing weapons. "We need to alert the guards. Colin and Madeline are under attack."

Pam Binder

Chapter Forty-Five

The boat was waiting, as well as a contingent of Colin's soldiers. Activity around the castle side of the island told Colin that more men were on their way. He drove the carriage as close to the shore as he dared and pulled on the reins. He handed them off to Gregor and jumped to the ground.

His soldiers had surrounded the carriage with their swords drawn. Unafraid, Madeline climbed out of the carriage. They'd had a harrowing ride, and most people, men or women, would have cowered in a corner or become hysterical. It was not that she appeared calm; it was that she looked like she was ready to tackle the challenge and help him in any way she could. If he had not already fallen in love with her, this would have been the defining moment.

He pulled Madeline behind him as Henry and his men approached. "It is over, cousin. Go home."

"When you relinquish your claim and your father declares me the Penrose heir, then and only then will this be over between us." Henry signaled to his men, and they turned to leave, galloping along the shore before making a sharp turn into the woods.

Madeline entwined her arm around his. "Henry is not leaving, is he?"

"No. we need to return to the castle and prepare for a siege."

****

Tintagel Castle loomed gray against the crimson ribbons of dawn. Madeline and Colin had been given horses when they arrived on Tintagel Island, a formidable fortress of rock and iron. Madeline tilted her head to take in the height of the towers shading her from the morning sun. They'd ridden for what seemed like hours, and she was bone tired. Colin had told her that the Romani would camp on Tintagel Island, and he planned to join them as soon as they were settled.

Shadows moved inside the narrow windows, giving the impression they were being watched. The island castle looked as cold and unwelcoming as the rocks used in its construction.

She shivered as her horse let out a breath that frosted the air. She leaned over her saddle to soothe him. "I'm afraid for the Romani, too," she whispered. Colin hadn't said his father might refuse to allow the Romani inside the castle walls, but Madeline could feel the strain in his voice every time it was mentioned.

Her goal had been to reach Tintagel Castle. They'd arrived, and now she wished she were back with the Romani. They were warm and welcoming, in direct contrast to this cold, hard island castle.

Chains and iron strained to open the drawbridge, grating against the sea-weathered stones. Two guards rushed from their post to greet Colin. Their welcome told Madeline that Colin was more than their lord's son; he was their comrade in arms. She overheard Colin ask about his father's health and noted the glances the guards exchanged with each other before responding. The message was clear. Colin's father's injuries weren't healing as well as Colin had hoped.

Colin gave instructions to send a contingent of soldiers to help the Romani when they arrived and then report back to him on their progress. What was left unsaid was that Colin wanted his soldiers to help protect the Romani if they were attacked.

The man who had been so easy to talk to earlier had now retreated into the dark place he'd been in when he was in the barn in Glastonbury. It was as though the shadows that spread over the castle held Colin in their grasp.

"Do you think the Romani will be all right?" Madeline said.

"They are some of the best fighters I have ever known. I told Stefan before we left that if he ran into trouble, he and the Romani could shelter within the walls of Tintagel Castle."

He maneuvered his horse next to hers, facing her and taking her hand. "You care for the Romani."

"Of course. Why wouldn't I? They are a gentle and kind people and are protecting the women accused of witchcraft, even though their actions place them in danger. Not everyone would do that. That is a very brave thing to do."

"You risked your life as well," he pointed out, rubbing his thumb over the knuckles of her hand.

His touch chased away the gloom and lifted her heart. "So did you," Madeline said.

Colin pulled her hand to his lips and brushed a kiss against her skin. "You helped me right an injustice. I am in your debt. For too long I have thought only of myself and this blessed castle. You challenged me to think of others, and for that I am grateful beyond measure."

He was too hard on himself. His capacity to care for others had also been part of him. "You have a right to think about your castle and your obligations. I'm sure your father will be pleased when he learns you found Excalibur."

"*We* found Excalibur," he said. "My father will be pleased when I marry. But I am more committed than ever. I will marry only for love."

She loved that he recognized her role. It fueled her building theory that there were men in this century who respected women and considered them their equals. "Believe me, I understand about family obligations. It's probably hard for your father to understand love. Sir Thomas Malory's book *The Death of Arthur*, that romanticized the concept, was published only a short time ago."

He smiled, leaning closer. "You could find flowers growing at the site of a ruin. Have you always looked on the bright side of life?"

"It is something you are teaching me."

Colin brought her hand to his lips and kissed it. "Then we are good for each other, and I would argue that there has been love since the dawn of time. Malory just gave it a voice." He rose on his saddle and leaned toward her. His kiss was whisper-soft, but the fire it contained shimmered over her skin like the touch of the sun.

"Colin," she managed through parted lips, "we are being watched."

"I hope so." He motioned toward the tower above them. "I have no doubt that word of our arrival has spread throughout the castle by now, and our kiss will announce, more than words, my feelings for you. The message is clear. The Penrose heir is in love."

Her heart sang with his declaration. "You kissed me on purpose."

"Always." His eyes held mischief as he turned his horse. "It is time we meet my father."

Chapter Forty-Six

Colin's words made her feel as though she were sailing on a cloud instead of sitting on the back of a jolting horse. Even the statement that he would introduce her to his father had not dimmed her spirits. From all accounts, his father was hard and judgmental. It occurred to her that she had described her father in the same way.

Keeping a safe distance behind Colin, Madeline followed him under the raised gate and into a tunnel lit by torches lining the stone walls. Her mother had taken her to Europe when she'd graduated from high school. She'd lost track of how many castles they'd visited and joked to friends that in Europe they'd learned their ABCs. ABC was their code for Another Bloody Castle.

The tunnel opened into a walled courtyard. The look and feel reminded her of the one she and her mother had visited in Edinburgh, Scotland, that perched on an extinct volcano. From the castle's vantage point, it could defend the city from attack, and like Tintagel, it was more of a fortress than a residence for the king and his court.

A breeze, kissed by salt-sea air, ruffled Madeline's hair. She brushed strands from her face, breathing deeply. Seagulls cawed overhead as they wheeled and landed on the turrets and windowsills. Like the ravens at the Tower of London, the birds watched over the castle. Seagulls were as numerous as coffee houses were in Seattle, and their presence helped diminish the unwelcoming feel she'd had moments before. These birds hunted and fished, fought over bits of food, and perched on rocks on the castle wall. In her century, they would do exactly the same thing. Like the seagulls, people weren't that much different in the future from those now. They wanted to take care of their families, develop friendships, and find love.

Colin dismounted and was greeted by a man about his age, except that was where the similarity ended. The man was clean shaven, looked like he had a rod up his back, and was in a constant state of anger. The tone of their conversation matched the man's expression. When the man stomped away, Colin returned to help Madeline dismount.

Her euphoria slipped a little. "Who were you talking to? Is it about your father? Is he all right?"

Colin ground out his words. "The man's name is Douglas. He said nothing about my father other than that he has sent our guests home. Douglas was too busy asking questions about who you are and where I have been over the past few days."

"What did you tell him?"

"I told him it was none of his business."

Madeline laughed. "Good for you. You should visit your father. He will be expecting you, and I can make myself comfortable inside." She wasn't sure how she was going to keep that promise, but the last thing she wanted was for Colin to worry about her.

He shook his head. "We will see my father together. I need you with me."

With all the reasons he could have given, that was

the one that reached her heart. She gave a small nod and let him lead her up the stone stairs and through the double doors.

The interior of the castle reflected the fortress-like austerity of the exterior. Gray stone walls, damp from the sea air, rose from the ground like the Cliffs of Moher in Ireland. Torches blazed, sending spirals of smoke into the air. The hall was bare, with the exception of a display of weapons and shields on the wall opposite the staircase. Everywhere were sharp corners and the cold images of war. The absence of the touches that make a house a home was glaring.

The lack of color and warmth shook her to her core. How could a child feel love in such a place? She cast a sidelong glance toward Colin. And yet he was filled with kindness, loyalty, and the desire to help others. Her heart swelled, marveling at the man he'd become despite the coldness of his environment.

In silence, Madeline climbed the stone stairs to the second floor. When they reached the top floor, Colin paused.

She wrapped her arm through his, leaning against his shoulder. "No matter what your father says or how he greets you, promise me that you will tell him you love him."

His eyes hooded in confusion. "My father would view it as a weakness. He believes love hurts."

She reached up and touched Colin's beard, pulling on it gently. "You told me he still mourns the death of your mother. Your father believes in love, and I'm sure he loves you. My guess is that he's forgotten how to express his feelings."

"Sire," a servant said, interrupting. "Your father

has been informed of your arrival and wishes to see you."

Lord Penrose's bedchamber was as austere as the rest of the castle. The only nod to the lord's exalted position was a four-poster bed hung with gold velvet draperies. The air was stale, and the windows shuttered closed. Madeline resisted the impulse to throw open the windows and let in fresh air. She was fully aware that her actions would be considered odd. She needed to blend in, not stand out. In the fifteenth century, fresh air was considered dangerous. In some cases, the idea was not that far off. The plague was an airborne disease, and after over three centuries of death and heartache, it had been defeated only when the human race developed a natural immunity to the epidemic.

The fragile-looking man in the bed opened bloodshot eyes. "What are you doing here? I told you I never wanted to see you again."

The angry words hung in the air. What struck Madeline was that Colin did not seem surprised by his father's outburst. This was unfinished business between father and son, and she needed to make herself scarce.

She kissed Colin on the cheek. "I'll leave you and your father alone. Remember, he's your father. I'll wait outside."

"Madeline, I want you with me."

She smoothed her hand across his chest, feeling the warmth of his words. "It's important you settle whatever is between the two of you. I'm not going anywhere." The words tumbled out and brushed over her skin like a promise, and with all her heart she wanted them to be true.

Chapter Forty-Seven

"Did you hear me, son?" Colin's father raged. "I told you to leave."

The air, stale and rotting, reached out to surround Colin. He stood his ground against the familiar stench. He had spent his life ignoring his demons. It was time to face them. His mother had died giving him life.

His father's face was flushed, and the expression in his eyes a challenge. Under the anger, Colin recognized other emotions: deep hurt, vulnerability, and the loss of hope.

The last time he and his father had spoken was on the day he left for Glastonbury. It felt as though years had passed instead of days. In the heat of their anger, Colin had refused to consider that his father fought his own demons.

"I visited the Romani," Colin said.

Colin's words seemed to disturb the currents in the air around his father. The man's gaze darted around the room, then settled on Colin. His father moved higher on the mountain of pillows at his back and winced, bit back a groan, and said, "You were forbidden." His voice held a trace of steel, a reminder of the man he'd once been. "Repeatedly."

"I know," Colin said.

"Your mother loved them too." His voice deflated to reed-thin.

The air shifted as though a breeze had slipped through the spaces between the shutters as Colin approached the bed slowly.

"Please tell me about my mother," Colin said.

When he was a child, he had asked the same question many times, always with the same response. His father had said there was nothing to tell and had changed the subject. Colin pulled a chair beside the bed, trying to read the emotions on the drawn expression of the man lying before him.

His father's eyes pooled with tears. He flattened the blankets over his chest. "Your mother, Catherine, was the most beautiful woman I had ever seen in my life. Her hair was as black as night and like liquid silk against my hands. Her laughter and her good heart brought life back into this dreary castle. The matchmaker said she was Romani, which accounted for Catherine's odd speech and unfamiliarity with English customs. At Catherine's request, I invited the Romani to the wedding. The priest in Glastonbury told me he would not marry us if the Romani were present. I had to send them away. I did not have a choice." He took in a deep breath and cried out in pain, doubled over, only to moan again.

As much as Colin wanted to learn more, he did not press his father. The man was in pain. Colin wiped the sweat from his father's brow with a cloth. "Father, you need your rest. If your physicians can no longer help you, I will send for Aunty Florica. She is the Romani's best healer."

His father pushed the cloth away. "You have your mother's eyes. They also reflected her emotions. Do not worry about me, son. I am in God's hands now."

Colin drew back, dropping the cloth. That was the first time his father had remarked on any similarity. It made him feel closer to his mother somehow, a real connection that went beyond knowing that his mother had given him birth.

"I was a fool and buried in grief after Catherine died. I had all paintings of her destroyed. I thought that if they were gone, I could forget the way she looked and the way she made me feel each time she smiled at me or laughed when I brought her a flower from the garden we had planted together. I had forgotten, however, that unique accent of hers until I overheard you talking to the woman you brought to the castle. What is her name?"

"Madeline."

"Madeline," his father repeated slowly. "Did she mention where in the future she is from? Your mother was from the twentieth century."

Chapter Forty-Eight

Madeline retraced her steps down the long narrow corridor. She'd heard Colin and his father arguing and wanted to give them privacy. Relationships between children and their parents were complicated. She'd experienced that firsthand. The parent clung to his or her way of doing things and the child wanted change.

She reached the staircase, imagining what it would look like if the oak banisters were draped with Christmas garlands and twinkling lights. The castle reminded her of a five-tiered wedding cake before all the sugar roses were added. Her mother would have fun transforming the gray walls, arranging poinsettia plants, and tucking sprigs of holly in every nook and cranny. Her mother had a flair for seeing the potential in both people and things. Was that what had first attracted her mother to her father? Had she seen something in him that he'd kept hidden?

Whatever it was, it hadn't worked out. They were too different—her mother was spontaneous, and her father liked order—and neither of them was willing to change or compromise.

Madeline wandered into a small room, just off the entrance, that looked out over a narrow channel of water separating the castle from the mainland. She supposed she had a little of both of her parents' qualities in her. Her parents were good people who wanted what all parents wanted, for their child or children to be happy, and believed as all parents did that they knew how to accomplish that goal.

After all, they had the experience of parenthood, changing their child's diapers, helping them with their homework, being there to pick them up when they fell down. The logical next step would be to assume they could orchestrate a happily-ever-after for their child.

Madeline laughed aloud. She should have seen this before. Her parents, each in their own way, believed their advice would result in their child's happiness. When she returned, she'd thank them but let them know it was also time for them to let go.

"I heard laughter," a woman said, holding out her hand in greeting as she entered the room. "I'm the matchmaker Fiona, and I assume you are Madeline."

Fiona's smile lit up her face. It was the kind of smile that made you want to smile in return, no matter the type of day you were having. Fiona's gown was candle-flame gold and reflected the color of her shoulder-length hair. Both gown and hair shimmered as she approached. One hand was outstretched toward Madeline, and the other rested on the slight mound of her belly.

"Nessa arranged for me to meet you at the Thistle Down Inn." She smiled softly, rubbing her belly. "I had morning sickness and was searching for what passes for a restroom in this century when you arrived. When I realized we'd missed each other, I sent my husband, Liam, to search for you. It looks as though things worked out. You found Colin on your own. Is he with his father?"

A seagull perched on the ledge outside the leaded

glass window and blinked at Madeline as though it were watching over her. Madeline had no reason to distrust Fiona, and yet... Fiona had sent Liam to look for her. Lady Roselyn had not wanted Madeline to time travel. Did Fiona feel the same way? Had Fiona sent Liam to look for Madeline with the intention of sending her back?

Madeline tapped on the windowpane, and the bird bobbled her head, spread her wings, and glided toward the mainland. "I talked with Nessa," Madeline said, gauging Fiona's reaction.

Fiona's good mood crumbled. "I regret the part I played. Nessa should not have sent you here."

Chapter Forty-Nine

His father must be mad to suggest that his mother and Madeline were from a future time.

Colin threw open the windows in his father's bedroom. A salt-sea breeze swept in to cleanse and cool the air. He had heard that when some people aged, their memories could become confused and their minds forgetful, even delusional. His father believed Colin's mother and Madeline were from the future. Impossible.

What, or who, had convinced his father to believe in such a tall tale? There were legends in Ireland of people disappearing into the fairy realms only to reappear years later the same age as when they had left. It was a child's bedtime story, nothing more.

The vast steel-gray ocean stretched out to the horizon and beyond, its surface benign one day and angry the next, housing a hidden world of monsters that tested the bounds of the imagination. It was not that long ago that men believed the world was flat and a ship could sail off the edge. Was the concept that a person could travel back in time that much harder to grasp than the roundness of the earth?

"Son, come away from the window."

Colin did as his father asked. He did not want to believe his father was mad, but what other conclusion could there be? His thoughts were in turmoil.

"Father, please explain what you meant when you

said that my mother and Madeline are from a different century, a different time than ours."

His father sank lower under the bedcovers and pulled them over his shoulders. He yawned. "Matchmaker Nessa explained the meaning of the phrase of the curse that says, 'a woman out of time.' Our ancestors believed it meant a woman almost too old to have a child. According to Nessa, that is not the case. 'Out of time' means a woman not from our present but from a different time either the future or the distant past. Catherine—and, I suspect, Madeline—are women from the future."

Colin rubbed the back of his neck, crossed to the bed, and pulled another blanket over his father. "'A woman from the future' sounds like a tale told around a campfire to keep the shadows at bay."

"It is not a story." His father's voice held an edge. "What I tell you is true. Ask Madeline, or the matchmaker Nessa. If only we had Excalibur." He yawned again as his eyelids drooped. "The Romani were convinced they could find it. I was a fool. I listened to the priest who said I had been bewitched by the Romani and ordered that I send them away. If I had not listened to him, perhaps my Catherine would still be alive." His eyes fluttered shut.

"Father..." Colin shook him gently. "Father, we found the sword." Loud snores rumbled in the chamber as his father slipped into a deep sleep. Had his father heard him?

He braced his hand against the bedpost. How could his father's theory be true? Would Madeline think him mad for believing such a story? Was Colin so desperate to want Madeline to satisfy the curse that he would suspend logic?

He pushed away from the bedpost and took a deep breath. He did not need to embrace his father's theory. Madeline and he were the same age, which according to his ancestors already qualified her as a woman out of time.

What his father said was not possible. Then again, if it were... He had to find Madeline. He had to ask her if what his father said was true. Colin made sure his father rested comfortably, then left the chamber, shutting the door behind him.

He plowed into Douglas.

Douglas looked like he was bracing for confrontation. Whatever had Douglas on edge would have to wait.

"If you are here to visit my father," Colin said, "he is sleeping."

Douglas blocked his path. "The Romani are a plague on the earth."

Colin walked past Douglas as he headed toward the stairs, looking for Madeline. Colin had heard the same tired argument from Douglas before and was not in the mood to spar with him. "Not now, Douglas," he said over his shoulder. "Please let the servants know that my father wishes to have the King's room prepared for Madeline. Do you know where she is?"

"She is with them." Douglas' voice was filled with venom.

Colin stopped short. "With whom?"

"The Romani. Haven't you been listening to me? They are here. They arrived shortly after you went in to visit with your father. For some reason, they believe they are welcome at Tintagel Castle."

Colin turned on Douglas, his voice as hard as steel. "They *are* welcome here."

Leaving Douglas fuming, Colin raced down the stairs. In the entry, Stefan, Aunty Florica, and half a dozen Romani men, women, and children were gathered around Madeline. She held onto the hand of a little girl.

Madeline spotted him first. Releasing the child's hand, she rushed over to him. "Colin! Oh, good, you're here. Just in time. Douglas said the Romani aren't welcome to stay in the castle. I told him you were explaining the situation to your father."

Her smile brought sunshine to the shadows. His father had said something similar about Catherine. Colin wished his father had shared more. His wound must be deep to have kept it hidden for so long. For the first time, Colin's heart softened toward his father. He had only known Madeline a short time, but if he lost her it would break his heart.

He wanted to ask her if his father's claim that she was from the future was true or just the ramblings of an old man. To be honest, he had been so pleased to see her again that he had not asked her where she had been for the past year or why she had appeared back in his life so suddenly. And did any of it matter?

The little girl skipped over to Colin and held up her hands toward him. He picked her up and swung her around in a circle, producing a chorus of giggles. Laughing, he set the little girl down beside Madeline. If there was magic in the world, it was in the smiles of the people he loved.

"The Romani are welcome here," he said to Stefan. "You are safer inside these walls. I will inform the guards to open the gates when the rest of the wagons arrive."

"Your father has changed his mind about us?" Stefan said.

"I did not ask his permission. The Romani need shelter, and it is the right thing to do."

"How is your father?" Madeline asked.

"Confused and in need of a healer for both his mind and his body."

Aunty Florica approached and burst into a hearty laugh. "Your father sounds the same as when we first met."

He smiled. Her assessment brought a much-needed lighter mood. He had forgotten that the two of them had known each other for a long time. "Granted, my father is not an easy man. It would be a great favor to me if you would see to his care."

"If the stubborn mule will see me. We did not part on the best of terms. I may have called him a murderer."

Pieces of the conversation he had with his father fell into place. "He will see you now, I promise. He is a man in need of healing."

Stefan clasped Colin on the shoulder. "We all are, my friend. We all are."

Chapter Fifty

Hours later, Madeline stood in the most opulent bedchamber she'd ever seen, and she'd visited Versailles. The contrast between Lord Penrose's bedchamber and this room would be like comparing jogging shoes to a pair of designer heels. She and Colin had made sure the Romani were settled comfortably in a wing of the castle, and then Colin had escorted Aunty Florica to his father's chamber. Colin had been uncharacteristically quiet, as though distracted. She completely understood. He had a lot on his mind.

The witch hunters would not give up. The only question was if they were bold enough to attack a fortified castle. She'd traveled back in time to experience a taste of this century. She knew warfare was part of the Late Middle Ages and the Early Renaissance period in the abstract way she'd also read about women and men being falsely accused of witchcraft. Experiencing it firsthand had brought out the true horror.

The people she'd met were survivors. They faced their life-and-death challenges head-on and with courage. She complained when a barista confused her latté order. Life and its challenges could always use perspective.

She'd agreed to this adventure because she'd have a better chance with a man from the past than with a contemporary. To paraphrase an old proverb, wherever you went, you took yourself with you. The adventure hadn't so much helped her find someone she could love as it had shed light on the person she wanted to be.

And if she wanted the relationship with Colin to work, she had to be honest with him, regardless of the consequences. Being from the future was part of who she was. He was attracted to her because she was strong and outspoken and different from other women he knew. He had saved the three women from the witch hunters. She was about to test how tolerant he was when she told him she was from the future. Even if he believed her, would the concept be so strange to him that he would turn her over to the witch hunters?

It was a risk she had to take.

Feeling as though the walls were closing in around her, she crossed to the bed in the center of the room.

It was the size of two king-sized beds, with a heavy tapestry cover whose embroidery depicted scenes of an enchanted forest. The four posts were carved to resemble twisting vines of ivy where multicolored butterflies, with pearl and emerald wings, played hide-and-seek amongst the leaves.

She sat on the bed and smoothed her hand over the velvet-soft cover. She traced her fingers over the image of a gold hummingbird with a red ruby beak. What she avoided looking at too closely was her fantasy of what it would be like to be Colin's wife. She wanted to be with him even if it meant living her life here at the end of the fifteenth century.

She wouldn't miss the Internet. Hot and cold running water might be an issue. And she was pretty sure chocolate hadn't made it to Europe yet. Cortez had to sail to South America and bring cocoa beans back to Spain first.

What was she thinking? Even if Colin accepted that she'd time traveled, could she live here? This wouldn't be like attending a Renaissance or medieval fair. She couldn't leave whenever she wanted, and navigating through the obstacle course of surviving these times had disaster written all over it. She shook her head to clear her fantasies.

Would love be enough?

Chapter Fifty-One

"What is that woman doing here?" Colin's father shouted, his voice stronger than it had been in days.

Colin kept his voice calm, though he wanted to shake sense into his father. "Aunty Florica has offered to heal you."

"That woman called me a murderer."

Aunty Florica winked at Colin. "I told you." She walked toward the bed. "Well, well, at least your father still has his memory. What is wrong with him besides his smell and bad temper? And could you open the windows? There is no air in this chamber. It's closed tighter than your father's mind."

"And your tongue is as sharp as the day we first met. Colin, make her leave."

"I'm not leaving, you crusty old goat. Colin asked me to heal you. Colin, how was he injured?"

His father balled his fists in his lap. "Why don't you ask me, you skinny sorceress?"

"Because I need the truth, John."

Aunty Florica smelled the water beside John's bed and wrinkled her nose. "You need fresh water and linens."

Colin crossed to the windows and lifted the wood bar that kept the shutters in place. Aunty Florica and his father bickered like old friends. He was glad he had asked her help. "My father fell from his horse and broke his leg, as well as a few ribs. The physician sent by the priest in Glastonbury bound his ribs and set his leg. But the physician suspected internal bleeding and recommended we send for the priest to administer the last rites."

"An infection might account for the smell." Aunty Florica put her wrist to John's forehead and lifted the blanket over his legs with her other hand.

John snatched the blanket out of Aunty Florica's grasp and covered his legs again. "What are you doing, woman? Have you no shame or decency?"

She perched her hands on her hips and turned toward Colin. "Tell your father that I have buried two husbands, and there is nothing he has that I have not seen before. Beyond that, he has a slight fever, and his leg is infected. I'll want to change the dressing on his leg and rebind his chest. There are fine physicians in London, but whoever tended to your father was no healer. Fetch fresh linens and a tub for a hot bath, and I'll need my satchel of herbs."

His father pushed out his chin and pouted. "Bossy woman. You were not like this when we were younger."

Her eyes softened. "When we were younger, you were different as well."

He turned his head away. "All I am saying is that I will not have you using your rotting herbs on me."

Aunty Florica emptied the water jug out the window and gave Colin a smile. "Tell your father that I use only the freshest pigs' balls and rats' tails in my potions."

"I heard that, Florica," John muttered. "Stop talking about me behind my back."

Aunty Florica whirled on him. "I'll stop talking behind your back, John, if you explain why you drove the Romani away. We could have helped. Instead, you turned your back on us—on me, when you needed us the most."

He squeezed his eyes shut and moaned, "I blame the matchmaker Nessa. If she had not brought Catherine into my life…"

Aunty Florica pursed her lips together. "If not for Catherine, Colin would not have been born. What choice did Nessa have but to seek a woman unfamiliar with your family's history? Only then might a woman give love a chance. Nessa assured us she knew the location of Excalibur, yet you sent us away before we could find it."

"I was confused and made the mistake of confessing to a priest from Glastonbury about the plans to get Excalibur. He called time travel dark magic."

Colin swore under his breath. He had thought Aunty Florica's presence would help clear his father's mind of such fantastical imaginings. Her presence only made it worse. "Father, calm yourself. Time travel is not possible."

"Oh, but it is," Aunty Florica said. "And if you are honest with yourself, you know that you suspected something different about Madeline from the beginning."

"I never believed Nessa," John said as though to himself. "Nessa claimed Catherine was from the future. The priest told me that if Catherine and I wanted happiness and eternal life in heaven, we must cut all ties with the Romani and never speak of it again."

Anger slammed against Colin's chest with such

force he stepped back. The Church's fear of what they did not understand had caused his mother's death as sure as if it had wielded the weapon that killed her. His father was as much a victim as his mother had been. His father had trusted the priest's superstitious lies.

When his father realized he had been betrayed, the guilt must have threatened to consume him. "Father..."

John's shoulders hunched over as he held his head in his hands and rocked back and forth slowly. "Son, I am so sorry. It was my fault your mother died."

Aunty Florica rushed over to his bedside and cradled John against her. "John, you did what you thought was right."

"I loved her," he sobbed.

Aunty Florica looked toward Colin. "Time-travel magic is beyond my knowledge, but I promise you, it is not dark magic. And like your mother, Madeline is also from the future. I had hoped she would tell you on her own, but she is afraid, and we are running out of time. Go to her. Do not judge. Your mother traveled to this century to find love, and so has Madeline. If it is in your heart to do so, tell her she made the right decision."

Chapter Fifty-Two

Madeline awoke to the smell of fresh bread. She'd slept only for a short time, but she felt refreshed. She stretched and padded over to the table. A servant had slipped in while she slept and laid out a feast on a silver tray. She'd read enough historical novels to know that servants entered rooms from hidden passageways. Still, it was a little creepy that someone had been in her room while she slept.

Her stomach grumbled that she should eat now and freak out later. There was fresh bread, a hard, white cheese, butter, and an assortment of sliced meats. Her mouth watered as she slathered a slice of bread with butter.

A knock on the door was followed by Colin's request to enter. With her mouth full of bread, she opened the door to let him inside. "The food is delicious," she said through her mouthful. "You should have some. Especially the bread. I could live on this bread. I've never tasted anything this good before."

He gave her a questioning glance before he headed toward the hearth. "I am not hungry."

"That's a first," she said, and cut around him to make a sandwich of the bread and cheese. "How's your father?"

"Aunty Florica is with him now." Colin gave a weak smile. "She told him he smelled and ordered he take a bath."

Madeline chuckled and perched on the side of the bed. "I wish I could have seen your father's expression. Aunty Florica is fierce."

Colin's eyebrow arched higher. "Fierce? You have used the word before. What is its meaning?"

"You know—tough, fearless...fierce."

He nodded. "You have many words and expressions that are unfamiliar to me."

Madeline settled higher on the bed. Colin was distracted. Maybe if she kept talking, he'd open up to her. "Why doesn't your father use this room?" she said. "It's gorgeous. And this bed... There are seven mattresses. I counted. No wonder it's so soft. Even the princess from the fable *The Princess and the Pea* would be comfortable in this bed."

"Excuse me?"

"Never mind. I'm just making small talk."

His eyebrow rose again. "Small talk?"

"An expression meaning words to fill an awkward silence."

He gave a quick nod, then began to pace a trail through the rushes and lavender strewn on the floor, his steps sending a soft, spring fragrance dancing through the air. "The bed is meant for a king or one of the nobles at court, in the hope they might visit our castle." His voice was flat. "As of yet, our invitations have been declined. Nonetheless, the servants are ordered to change the bedding and refresh the rushes every fortnight in case there is a surprise visit. If the King, or a member of his court, honored us with a visit, it would automatically expand the power and influence of our family." His voice elevated and held an edge. "My father spent a year's profits on this bed."

There was something on Colin's mind. Was it his father? Had his health deteriorated? "Be sure to thank your father for me." She wanted to offer to thank him herself, but changed her mind. There was tension between father and son, and regardless of his father's offering her this room, she wasn't sure she was welcome here.

He stopped pacing and turned toward Madeline, pain clouding his expression. "Is it true? Did you travel from the future like my mother?"

Colin knew.

He didn't seem angry or confused. He seemed hurt. "Let me explain," Madeline said, holding out her hands. "I wanted to tell you."

Wind rattled the shutters over the windows. One broke loose from its latch, swung open, and slammed against the wall. The force cracked the wood, but it held together.

Madeline jumped and brushed her hands over her arms. Outside, over the ocean, a storm built that rivaled the one inside.

Colin worked to secure the shutter as a muscle pulsed on his temple. He banged the shutter closed. "Why didn't you tell me you were from the future? Were you afraid I was like those witch hunters in the village who condemned what they did not understand? Although I was born within Tintagel's castle walls, I spent much of my life with the Romani. They taught me to look into a person's heart and leave judgment to God."

"You're right. I should have trusted you. I'm sorry. I'm still wrapping my own head around the fact that I time traveled. Time travel is considered science fiction or fantasy in my century, which is just another way of saying magic. I don't know how the matchmakers do it. All I know is that I walked over a threshold into your world, as simply as you walk from the doorway of the castle to the courtyard. Then, in a cloud of mist, I was standing in the Thistle Down Inn in the fifteenth century."

Colin gave a short laugh and moved closer to Madeline. "A year ago, Nessa approached me and guaranteed she could find me a match. We met in Glastonbury at a manor house and she opened a door, and that is when I met you." His smile broadened. "It appears I time traveled to your century." He paused and took her in his arms. "You came looking for me."

She grinned. "Finally, my Christmas Knight gets it. It was your fault. Gran took a liking to you and insisted that I bring you to my mother's wedding."

He kissed her forehead and whispered against her skin, "I must thank your grandmother. She is well, then?"

"Very. She's probably worried I won't keep my promise. My mother's wedding is on Christmas Eve."

Colin dropped his arms to his side and turned away to face the hearth. A log shifted in the firebox, and he used an iron poker to shove it back into place. "Christmas Eve is tomorrow night," he said evenly.

The tension in his eyes returned, and she didn't blame him. There was a lot for Colin to process. She had her own issues to process. In a short period of time, he had become her world. She had lost track of time and hadn't thought about her mother's wedding or how her mother would feel if she wasn't there—sad, frustrated, angry. Did he believe that she planned to leave to attend her mother's wedding and not return? Was that the reason his good mood had shifted? She had agreed to marry him and make his century hers. That hadn't changed. But not attending her mother's wedding was unthinkable.

She knelt down beside him. "How about this? I'll ask Nessa if it's possible for me to time travel to my mother's wedding, and the day after, on Christmas Day, I'll return, and we can plan our wedding and our lives together. That will give me the opportunity to explain the situation to my family."

He threw a log on the fire. "We were to be married on Christmas Eve. With the help of the Romani, my father has begun the preparations. If you have changed your mind, you can tell me. I will understand."

She looped her arm though his and leaned her head on his shoulder. He said he would understand, except she heard the hurt in his voice. If the circumstances were reversed, she would feel betrayed as well. "You are my world now. We will marry as planned. Nessa can take a message to my family."

The words hollowed out her heart. She was surprised how much it hurt. She prayed her family would understand.

Chapter Fifty-Three

The morning of Christmas Eve dawned to six inches of new snow and overcast gray skies. The castle prepared for both a siege and a wedding. Madeline wondered how her mother would have decorated for such an event. No doubt she would have discovered a way to make sure the bride received her dream wedding even while soldiers prepared for battle.

It was Madeline's turn to pace the King's bedchamber, and she told herself all brides were nervous on the day they were to get married. She wondered how her mother was doing today. She was also a bride preparing for her wedding.

Regret stabbed her in the stomach. She wouldn't be attending her mother's wedding, nor would her family be here for hers. She had to shake these thoughts or they would consume her. She needed to stay focused. She was getting married later today. Colin said Nessa and Fiona were decorating the chapel, and Aunty Florica was organizing the food. All she needed was the dress.

She opened the wardrobe. Dresses in an assortment of jewel tones hung in a row, from the deepest reds to meadow greens and blues. Normally she would be thrilled at the choices, but none was the color or style she wanted. She didn't want something this colorful. She wanted a champagne, or even a pale blush tone.

She wanted white.

A knock on the door interrupted her thoughts. Without waiting for Madeline to open the door, Nessa breezed in. Draped over her arms was a gown that shimmered like pearl dust. "I may have found you the perfect dress. Unless, of course, you're in love with those hideous gowns in the wardrobe."

Out of breath, Nessa spread the gown over the bed. Seed pearls covered the bodice and formed snowflake-like designs on the skirt and train.

"It's breathtaking," Madeline said, fingering the silk. "How did you know?"

"I'm a matchmaker. It's one of our gifts."

Madeline laughed as she spread the train over the embroidered bedspread. The contrast between the red-and-green bed covering and the winter-white dress's delicate beauty made her feel as though it was fit for a princess. "It's perfect."

Nessa gave Madeline a hug. "Don't worry. Everything will work out."

Madeline shivered. Was that what Nessa had said to Colin's mother the day she wed?

Chapter Fifty-Four

The controlled clap-clap of wooden practice swords filled the armory. Colin sidestepped Douglas's attack, executing one of his own. Douglas had suggested the idea, and Colin had wholeheartedly agreed. It helped distract him from the wedding. Madeline had not said anything, but he could tell it bothered her that her family would not be attending.

The monotonous sound of wood striking wood should have calmed him. It had the opposite effect. The sound grated. What was he doing? He was rushing Madeline into marriage in order to satisfy the conditions of the curse. Was that fair?

Douglas jabbed Colin in the arm with his practice sword. "You let down your guard."

"Good one." Colin blocked Douglas's next blow and drove him back.

It had been a long time since he and Douglas had sparred, trading stories and sharing dreams of the battles they would fight together. Those were uncomplicated, happier times, when adults made the decisions and he and Douglas believed they would live forever.

"You are getting married tonight." Practice sword raised, Douglas leapt toward Colin.

The accusatory tone in Douglas's voice caught Colin off guard. Regaining his calm, he blocked the attack and executed one of his own. The blow struck Douglas's sword, driving him back. "You sound disappointed," Colin said.

Douglas resumed his attack, increasing his pace. "You have always vowed never to marry. I am your best friend, yet a servant brought me the news." Douglas punctuated the last word with a thrust at Colin's chest.

Colin deflected the blow and sidestepped the next. Colin could end their match with a few well-positioned moves. He was the better swordsman. But his friend was angry for some reason, and as in the past, a mock battle helped Douglas regain his focus.

As Douglas had grown older, he had never shown interest in joining Colin on the battlefield, and at the order of Colin's father, no one pressured him about it. Some whispered that the lord felt guilty over how Douglas's father had died. Others considered it the duty of a soldier to defend his lord, regardless of the circumstances. Colin had asked Douglas about his father's dying words, but Douglas always changed the subject.

"Shall we break our exercise for a pint of ale?" Colin offered, wanting to end the contest. Instead of the match helping focus his friend, Douglas had grown more aggressive. Even with a practice sword, accidents could happen. His friend was no longer a young man. A sheen of sweat covered Douglas's heated face.

Douglas dropped his sword at his side, wiping his forehead with his sleeve. "You remain the better swordsman. One day, however, you will meet your match."

Colin flinched at the harsh words said in anger.

"That happens to us all, Douglas," Colin shot back.

"When you returned from Glastonbury, you brought a woman no one had ever met and introduced her as your betrothed. You must be confident you can break Merlin's Curse. Does that mean you not only found a woman who would marry you, but you also have Excalibur?"

At the mention of Madeline and Excalibur, Colin turned away. He considered placing his practice sword on the wall next to a wooden shield, then reconsidered. The edge to Douglas's voice had not eased. There had been a change in his friend over the last year that Colin did not understand. "I thought you would be happy that I am to marry."

Douglas snorted, his laugh hollow, hate dripping from his words. "Why would you think I would want you to marry and bring more cursed Penrose bastards into the world? My father's blind loyalty to your father killed him. I would not be as foolish. Father Patrick said that only a witch can break Merlin's Curse, and to align with a witch and those associated with them threatens our immortal souls."

Colin recognized the same fevered zeal he had witnessed in those who turned on the women he and Madeline had rescued in the village. Reasoning with Douglas would fall on deaf ears. Cautiously, so as not to startle Douglas, he circled forward. "What have you done?"

"I have assured my place in heaven. I informed Father Patrick about your witch. He plans to arrest her after the wedding ceremony."

Chapter Fifty-Five

The chapel was decorated like a forest wonderland. Bunches of plump red holly berries nestled in their shiny leaves were attached to each pew, and candles flicker from silver chandeliers. The room was packed with Romani and the people who lived in the castle.

Madeline stood in the center of the aisle that led to the altar, where Colin waited for her with the Romani priest. She loved the dress she wore. She loved how Nessa, Fiona, and Aunty Florica had decorated the chapel, and she loved Colin.

Everything was perfect. This should be the happiest day of her life.

Except it wasn't.

She'd always dreamed that her father would give her away on her big day. Gran would give her something borrowed and something blue, and her mother would be the one who would help her pick out her wedding dress and decorate the church. She took in a deep breath. She couldn't even show them pictures.

Aunty Florica came up beside her. "Have you changed your mind?" Yes, she wanted to scream. Instead she shook her head and concentrated on putting one foot in front of the other.

The ceremony blurred.

When the priest pronounced that she and Colin were man and wife, lightning flashed outside, and its burst of light illuminated the chapel in ribbons of silver. The ground trembled as something crashed to the ground and broke near where Colin's father stood. His shocked expression turned to joy, as he picked up the broken pieces and, with Aunty Florica's help, reached Colin's side.

"You did it, son. Against all odds, you did what I failed to do." He handed Colin the two halves of the broken plaque. "Merlin gave this to one of our ancestors when he issued his curse, with the message that when it broke that meant the terms of the curse were fulfilled. You returned Excalibur and married a woman out of time. I will gladly give you your inheritance. You have earned it."

Madeline spun on her heels. "Admit it! Marrying me was about money!" She twisted the ring on her finger, the ring Colin had just given her. It was set with a ruby surrounded by seed pearls and had belonged to Colin's mother. Would her own mother ever have a chance to see it? What had she done?

Her heart was breaking. "Was everything you said to me a lie? I should have known better. I knew this was happening too fast!" She picked up her skirts and ran.

Chapter Fifty-Six

Madeline ran along the cliff's pathway. Freezing rain poured from the night sky with its bruised shades of black and steel gray. Tears streamed down her face as she ran, and her rapid pace sent pebbles tumbling down the cliff to the whitecaps foaming below. Lightning flashed, illuminating the dark horizon and the ground beneath her feet. She was inches away from the edge. Heart racing and arms flailing to keep her balance, she stumbled back and collapsed to the ground. Thunder vibrated in the distance as though confirming how close she'd come to slipping over the edge of the cliff into oblivion.

She sucked in gulps of the ice-filled air as rain turned to sleet. She'd been caught up in the romance of the castle and a knight who took her breath away. She hadn't thought sensibly of what would happen to her in the days, months, and years after they wed. She'd wanted to believe he loved her as much as she loved him. She'd thought with her heart, not with her head. He'd wanted his inheritance and believed she was the person who could vanquish Merlin's Curse. He'd said he loved her. Words.

Her father had said those same words to the women he'd married over the years. In the end, it was never about love. It was because he didn't want to be alone.

In Colin's case, he considered their marriage a

business transaction.

She shivered and wrapped her arms around her waist, rocking back and forth. She wanted her old life back. A life she understood. A life of work and stress. A life devoid of love, with the inevitable heartache that accompanied failed relationships. She wanted to go home.

She rubbed the finger where Colin had placed the wedding ring. They were married and the curse broken. She had been swept up in the romance of it all and had never seriously questioned the speed with which it had all happened. She'd been a fool.

She rose on unsteady legs and stepped farther back from the edge. The castle loomed to her right, a dark image against a darker sky. A horse and rider galloped toward her. She straightened, feeling stronger since she'd made her decision. He would want her to stay. He would say all the right things and whisper the right terms of endearment. She brushed the tears and rain from her cheeks. He could marry again and fulfill his dream of filling the castle with children.

A sob caught in her throat.

Colin's horse skidded to a halt, and he jumped down and ran toward her, taking her in his arms, rubbing her shoulders, asking her if she was okay, asking her forgiveness. His voice sounded far away, as though it came from a great distance. She smiled, thinking of the irony. They were worlds apart. They had nothing in common.

He misinterpreted her smile, believing all was back the way it had been. She didn't try to convince him otherwise as he helped her onto the back of his horse and mounted behind her. She'd tell Fiona and Nessa her plan to return home and ask them to let Colin know that she'd left. She should tell him, of course, but leaving would take all her strength. It was best if she left as mysteriously as she'd appeared.

Best for whom? asked the voices in her head. But she didn't have an answer.

Chapter Fifty-Seven

Once inside the castle walls, Colin helped Madeline down from the horse and tried to pull her into an embrace.

A numbness washed over her. She'd made her decision. The sooner she returned to her own time, the better. She eased away from him. "It's cold. I think I'll go inside."

He reached for her hand. "Madeline. You have to believe me. I wanted to marry you because I love you. I do not care about the inheritance or this bloody castle. It has brought only heartache and tragedy to whoever possessed it. I care only about you."

She slipped her hand from his. A weight pressed down on her heart. "I don't belong in your world. I have to go."

Colin stepped in front of her. "If you want me to give it all up for you, I will. Just say the word."

She put her hand on his chest and felt the solid beat of his heart. "I will not ask that of you. You would be giving up your birthright, the wealth, the power."

"I do not care. It means nothing without you."

The bells began to toll. Armed soldiers ran to their posts on the walls as the drawbridge was raised.

"The castle is under attack," Colin said. "How did they manage to cross on the ferry to the island without our guards stopping them? I must get you to safety."

When they entered the castle, the sound of the bells and the shouts of men rang in her ears. Colin shouted orders. It would be a long siege. Well trained and prepared, everyone took their places. The sights and sounds buffeted Madeline on all sides.

Stefan appeared from a side entrance. He dragged Douglas behind him and shoved him to the ground. Stefan unsheathed his sword and pointed it at Douglas. "Tell Colin of your betrayal, you miserable coward."

"I did nothing wrong. I am protecting Tintagel from those who would defile its memory by allowing scum like you to inhabit these sacred walls, and its heir to install a witch as the Lady of Penrose."

Colin grabbed Douglas and dragged him to his feet. "This castle's history was defiled long before the Penrose family took possession. King Arthur was born here as the result of Merlin's treachery. If anything, Madeline and the Romani have helped breathe fresh air into its cursed walls." Colin shook Douglas. "Are you responsible for this attack?"

Douglas sneered. "I merely told your guards that Father Patrick and his men had come to celebrate your wedding."

"Do you hate the Romani and what they stand for so much that you would risk the lives of everyone in this castle? My father took you in after the death of your father and treated you like a son."

Blind hatred glowed red-hot in Douglas's eyes. "If not for your father, mine would still be alive. On his deathbed he told me that he regretted giving up his life to save your father's."

Colin released his hold on Douglas and stepped back.

"It would be my pleasure to escort Douglas to the dungeon," Stefan said.

"No. Escort him to the gate and release him into Father Patrick's care. I want him out of my sight."

Chapter Fifty-Eight

"Where are you taking me?" Madeline asked, fighting against Colin's grip on her hand. It felt as though everything was falling apart.

"To see Nessa and Fiona," Colin said.

He had left Stefan to take care of Douglas and was pulling her toward the ocean side of the castle. She lifted up the skirts of her long dress with her free hand to keep from tripping. He didn't stop his pace until he reached the weapons room on the ground floor. The room looked out over an expanse of never-ending ocean.

He released her hand. "You cannot stay here. With the castle under siege, it is not safe. There is no way to know how long the siege will last. Father Patrick has time on his side. He and his men can camp out in the woods and wait for us to run out of food. With me and my father dead, Henry will take possession of the castle. I will not put you in more danger. I have arranged it with Nessa. You have a way out. You can return to your own time."

The words settled in. A short time ago, leaving was what she had wanted. Now, with the castle surrounded by Colin's enemy, she knew she didn't want to leave him. Whatever happened, they would weather it together.

Nessa and Fiona stood on either side of a thick

241

wooden door studded with iron nails. Fiona opened the door, and mist rolled over the threshold.

Nessa walked toward Madeline. "Colin is doing the right thing, Madeline."

Madeline backed away. "Colin, come with me. I'm sure we can take your father, or anyone else who wants to leave."

Nessa and Fiona exchanged a glance, then both shook their heads.

"I must see this through to the end," Colin said. "My father has given Stefan authority to negotiate on our behalf. My father and I are as one voice on this. We do not want those who live in the castle to suffer."

A loud explosion split the air. Colin glanced over his shoulder. "They mean to burn the castle to the ground. I must help Stefan reach Father Patrick before people are hurt." He nodded toward Nessa.

Nessa and Fiona stood on either side of Madeline and pulled her across the threshold.

Madeline fought against them, but the women were much stronger than they appeared. Mist closed around her as she was forced through the portal.

Freezing rain fell from the cloud-soaked sky. Waves attacked the shore below, and somewhere in the distance a seagull announced his presence. Madeline shivered and pushed to her feet as relief washed over her. She was still on Tintagel Island. Nessa and Fiona must have pushed her over the wrong threshold. She would go back inside the castle and convince Colin to let her stay.

Teeth chattering, she turned. Castle ruins rose up before her, slate gray against a moonless night. Its walls were battered and broken from centuries of battles and neglect. Her heart sank. She had returned to her own time.

Nessa emerged from a stone archway shrouded in mist and the faint hum of distant music, and walked toward Madeline with slow even steps.

Madeline rushed to her and grabbed her by the shoulders. "You have to send me back. I love Colin. Isn't that what you wanted all along? This doesn't make any sense. I want to be with him, no matter what happens. I have to return."

"You can't now. It is not safe for a woman to time travel when she is pregnant."

Chapter Fifty-Nine

Christmas Eve—One year later

Madeline fingered the gold band with the red ruby Colin had given her on their wedding day. Her mother said that time would heal the hurt. Madeline was still waiting. People said things like: "Keep busy and connect with friends and family." She'd followed their advice, but she missed him more every day. Her life was good, though. Perhaps not perfect, but good.

Sunshine glistened like diamonds over the snow-dusted office building in St. George's Square as Madeline finished her phone call. Setting up her private practice in the cozy retail village outside of Seattle had been a great decision. She loved the friendly and welcoming location. It was a few doors down from her mother's office and a short walk to her home on Front Street.

The slower pace and relaxed atmosphere suited not only her needs but her clients' as well. She specialized in defending people against misconduct in the workplace. She was also able to continue her *pro bono* work for those who couldn't afford an attorney.

She shoved the stone bracelets the Romani had given her farther up her wrist and checked the video monitor in the next room. She smiled. Everything was quiet and peaceful.

Gran ducked her head into Madeline's office. "I forgot to tell you this morning. You look adorable in your red dress today." Her cheery smile chased Madeline's melancholy away. "I notified all your clients that the office was officially closed until the first week in January and how to get a hold of us in case of an emergency."

Her grandmother had been a godsend. Since recovery from her hip surgery, it was as though she had a new interest in life. Gran had been a paralegal before she retired and had offered her help when Madeline announced her plans to open her own law office. Now Madeline didn't know what she would have done without her.

"Thank you, and you're looking pretty awesome yourself. Did the matchmakers finally convince you to go out with that nice man who brings us flowers from his floral shop every week?"

A rosy blush brightened Gran's face. "You sound like your mother. She's happily married and is bound and determined that I date. Imagine such a thing at my age."

Madeline checked the video monitor again. "You dating is very easy to imagine, and Mom and I will even help you pick out a dress. But first, let's close up for the day. Fingers crossed we have an uneventful holiday. Do you have plans tonight?"

Gran straightened the folders on Madeline's desk and filed them in the cabinet next to the bookshelf with Madeline's law books. "I'm baking up a batch of my Christmas cookies tonight. What about you? Would you like to come over, or do you have plans with that adorable young man you've been seeing for the past three months?"

Madeline slipped into her desk drawer a client's file she'd been working on and smiled, her heart warming as she thought of her little man. "Johnny's going to help me pick out a Christmas tree. Would you like to come along? We could make the cookies afterward."

The door in the reception area chimed.

Gran closed the file cabinet and went to greet a potential client who evidently hadn't read the Office Closed sign. Madeline checked her messages again to see if anything new had come in during the last few minutes.

Gran screamed.

"Are you okay?" Madeline called out.

"Better than okay," Gran, responded, her voice infused with excitement. "Madeline, you have a surprise visitor. A good one."

"I hope someone sent a cookie bouquet," Madeline said heading toward the door. "I'm starving—Colin!"

He stood framed in the doorway, his beard and hair trimmed, wearing jeans and a brown bomber jacket. He was every inch a twenty-first century man. Her heart hammered in her chest. She stood frozen. Was she dreaming? She had just been thinking about him.

"Colin," she repeated, her voice sounding far away. She felt lightheaded on her heels and pitched forward.

His long strides ate up the distance between them, and he caught her before she fell, sweeping her into his arms. His kiss was warm and urgent. Time wound backward to the first time he'd kissed her. It all rushed back. Every word. Every kiss. Every caress.

"You're here."

He grinned. "I am here. The Romani helped me find Nessa, and I convinced her that I needed to see you."

Gran cleared her throat and motioned to the back offices with both arms. "I'm going to check on you-know-who."

Madeline nodded, then turned again to Colin. "You're here," she repeated, as he put her down to stand on the floor. "How long can you stay? No, I don't want to know. You're here now, and that is all that matters."

Madeline drank in his appearance. There was a new scar over his eye, and one at the base of his neck. She blinked away her tears, looking at her hands entwined with his. "How is your father? Did you and your men defeat the soldiers? How much damage was done to your castle? And what about that horrible priest? What was his name?"

"Father Patrick. The battle did not last long. We had surprise reinforcements. The Church in Rome had been investigating Father Patrick for some time and were not pleased with what he had been doing in Glastonbury. They took him into custody and left us alone." Colin laughed, fingering a strand of her hair. "So many questions. I missed your questions and a million other things about you." Colin rubbed his thumb over the gold wedding band on Madeline's finger. "You still wear my ring."

"I've never taken it off." She traced her fingers over the scar on his neck. The wound had healed, but she wished she had been there.

"A lot of time has passed. I told you once that if you were mine, I would never let you go. I loved you

247

with all my heart and I love you still. I thought sending you back to your own time was the right thing to do in order to keep you safe. But I broke my promise."

She heard the unspoken question in his eyes. She thought of what might have happened if she had stayed, and the risks each of them would have taken. "You didn't lose me. You did the right thing by sending me back. My Gran once told me that time was an illusion and love the only reality. I never understood that saying until now. It feels as though no time has passed between us at all. I never took off the ring because in my heart we'll always be married. I love you too."

He pulled her close, his arms wrapping around her. "You asked me how long I planned to stay. I plan to stay for as long as you want me in your life."

She smiled into his beautiful eyes. "I will want you forever." She paused. "What about your father? Your castle?"

He placed a gentle kiss on her lips. "You are always thinking of others. My father, it seems, thought of Tintagel more as a prison than as a home and knew I felt the same, especially after you left. He did not want Henry to have it, so he gave it to Stefan. My father has surprised us all by announcing that he and Aunty Florica have planned on getting married."

"I knew it. I want all the details."

He cupped her face with both of his hands, his gaze intense. "Can it wait? I have missed you so much." His gaze traveled to the large picture windows and the people passing by with Christmas presents. "Is there someplace we can go that is more private?"

She looked into his open and honest expression. His love poured out to her, embracing her in its warmth.

"Come with me." She took him by the hand and led him toward the office next to hers. "We have the rest of our lives together. First, I want you to meet your son. I named him after your father." She smiled, squeezing his hand. "Johnny has your eyes."

A word about the author...

Pam Binder is an award-winning Amazon and *New York Times* bestselling author and conference speaker. Pam believes in smiles, Irish and Scottish myths, and (like Wonder Woman) the power of love.

Pam writes historical fiction, time travel, contemporary fiction, middle grade, and fantasy.

Visit her at:

Website: www.pambinder.com
Twitter: PamBinder183
Facebook: pam.binder.5
Pinterest: pbinder183

Thank you for purchasing
this publication of The Wild Rose Press, Inc.

For questions or more information
contact us at
info@thewildrosepress.com.

The Wild Rose Press, Inc.
www.thewildrosepress.com

To visit with authors of
The Wild Rose Press, Inc.
join our yahoo loop at
http://groups.yahoo.com/group/thewildrosepress/